"You were on r... last week."

Derek's mouth eased into a small, thoughtful smile as his gaze lifted somewhat, and he added, "Must be the hair." His blue eyes returned to hers.

Gia suddenly couldn't think straight enough to say anything. She was just too overwhelmed with the idea of him kissing her. Something that certainly had no place here and now, at work, in her office, with her dressed for much worse than casual Friday, and him being who he was...

And yet he was looking at her as if he might be thinking about it, too.

That couldn't be...

But he wasn't making small talk anymore. He was standing there—dashingly handsome in a suit that probably cost as much as her car—just looking into her eyes.

Then down at her mouth...

Her chin went up a fraction of an inch as she looked into those astonishingly blue eyes of his, and she was ready.

* * *

The Camdens of Colorado:
They've made a fortune in business.
Can they make it in the game of love?

TO CATCH
A CAMDEN

BY
VICTORIA PADE

MILLS
BOON

Published in Great Britain 2014
by Mills & Boon, an imprint of Harlequin (UK) Limited,
Eton House, 18-24 Paradise Road, Richmond, Surrey, TW9 1SR

© 2014 Victoria Pade

ISBN: 978-0-263-91295-1

23-0614

Victoria Pade is a *USA TODAY* bestselling author of numerous romance novels. She has two beautiful and talented daughters—Cori and Erin—and is a native of Colorado, where she lives and writes. A devoted chocolate lover, she's in search of the perfect chocolate-chip-cookie recipe.

For information about her latest and upcoming releases, visit Victoria Pade on Facebook—she would love to hear from you.

Chapter One

"This is a wonderful thing you're doing, Gia."

Gia Grant laughed uncomfortably at the compliment from the church pastor. "The Bronsons are wonderful people," she demurred. "I didn't know how tough it could get for the elderly until seeing the way things are for Larry and Marion. And thanks again for letting us use the church basement tonight to organize everything so we can get started."

"Of course. The Bronsons have been church members since my father was pastor here. We want to do all we can."

"That reminds me—thank your mom, too, for the cookies and the brownies and the cupcakes. I was surprised when the Bronsons wanted to come tonight—they just don't go out much—but it's turned into a rare social event for them. Complete with goodies," she added with a nod toward the opposite end of the big room, where the elderly couple who were her next-door neighbors were chatting with other members of the church.

Gia had launched a grassroots effort to help the Bronsons. They were on the verge of losing their house because their fixed income wasn't meeting the cost of living expense increases and the additional medical expenses mounting with their age.

After making several calls and searching the internet for help for them, she'd discovered there weren't a lot of options available to older people in their predicament.

But she couldn't just sit back and watch what was happening to them without doing something. So she'd spread the word in their surrounding neighborhood that help was needed.

Small business owners who knew the Bronsons had put out donation jars at their checkouts. The church had sounded the alarm in their newsletter, and Gia had persuaded a local news station to do a human-interest piece on them. It mentioned both the donation fund Gia had started for them and the need for manpower to do repairs and maintenance on their house.

Gia's highest hope was that she could raise enough money to keep the Bronsons out of foreclosure. If she couldn't do that, then she at least wanted to get the place in order so that it could be sold before that happened.

Tonight, neighbors, friends and church members had gathered to form a plan of action to spruce the place up, and now that the meeting was finished it had become a social hour. Gia was happy to see the eighty-nine-year-old Larry and his eighty-seven-year-old wife, Marion, enjoying themselves.

"I was also wondering if you might have dinner with me some night…" Pastor Brian said, interrupting her thoughts.

Gia had wondered if that was coming. Although she didn't belong to the Bronsons' church, the minister had asked to be part of her efforts to help the older couple, and that had meant seeing him here and there. He'd become more and more friendly over the past few weeks.

At first Gia had thought he was merely trying to entice another sheep into his flock. But then a personal undertone had developed when he talked to her and she'd begun to wonder if he was interested in her.

Thinking that he probably wasn't, she'd still considered what she might do if he asked her out.

At thirty-four, Pastor Brian was only three years older than she was. He was nice looking, with golden-blond hair and hazel eyes. And he certainly came equipped with the attributes she was determined to look for in a man from here on out—he was upstanding and honest. There wasn't so much as a hint of wrongdoing in any aspect of him—he was a minister, for crying out loud.

But the fact that he was the head of his church put a crimp in things. Not only wasn't Gia a member of his religion, his job brought with it obligations and duties that were an uncomfortable reminder of the family ties that had bound her ex-husband and caused her to take a backseat in his life.

Plus, even though it had been nearly a year since her divorce was final, she felt as if she was just beginning to catch her breath, and she wasn't ready to get into the whole dating thing again yet. With anyone.

And then there was the fact that she *was* divorced.

"Thanks for asking, Brian, but no," she answered. "I like you, I do. But right now just the thought of dating gives me the willies. And even if it didn't, I'm *divorced*. And your congregation is old-fashioned. I've overheard

Marion's church-lady friends talking about finding you a wife—"

"I'm surprised they haven't formed a committee. By now I think I've been introduced to every young single female they're even remotely related to."

"You haven't been introduced to the ones who are single through divorce, I can promise you that," Gia said. "Because believe me, when it comes to who they want to see you with, it isn't anyone with that in her background. In their eyes, that's damaged goods and definitely *not* a prospect for their Pastor Brian."

The minister smiled sheepishly. "Yeah, I told my folks I was going to ask you to dinner and they said the same thing," he admitted. "But it would only be dinner and I thought I might risk a little scandal...."

Oh, good, I could go from being a shut-out in-law to a church scandal, Gia thought.

"But I'm really not ready," she repeated honestly. "I'm just barely getting my being-single-again sea legs."

He shrugged. "It's okay. I just thought I'd ask—no harm, no foul. I'm still with you a hundred percent on this project to help Larry and Marion."

"Thank you. I appreciate that." Gia pointed at the restroom sign. "I'm headed to wash my hands—I got into something sticky." And had just avoided getting into something even stickier....

"Yeah, I think I'm ready for another cup of coffee myself," he said, leaving Gia free to go into the bathroom.

Safely behind a closed door, she went straight to the row of three sinks, breathing a sigh of relief now that that was over.

It hadn't been *too* awkward, she decided.

The minister had taken her rejection in stride, so she thought it would all be okay. She hoped it would all be okay. And at least she knew now that she hadn't been imagining things—because even as she'd thought he might be showing her undue interest, she'd also wondered if she was flattering herself.

She washed her hands and took stock of her reflection in the mirror above the sinks. Dark eyes. Decent skin. An okay nose—not too prominent, not misshapen. A mouth she was afraid might be too wide, especially when she smiled. And dark, curly, curly—*really curly*—hair that she had to keep six inches below her shoulders so the weight of it would keep it from bushing out like a fright wig.

A neglectful husband—whose eye had begun to wander at the end of their marriage—and then a divorce had her making more assessments of her looks than she had since she was a teenager. And finding flaws. So even as she'd thought the pastor might have been showing her undue interest, she'd also been skeptical of the possibility that she *could* attract a man's attention.

Of course, there was also the fact that she was only five feet three inches tall—that made her one of the few people the five feet five inch minister was taller than....

That was probably the real reason, she thought suddenly, doubting herself all over again.

Gia's second sigh was a bit demoralized.

Oh, well. At least she could say she'd been asked.

She finished washing her hands and after drying them with a paper towel, she used the towel to brush wrinkles from the black slacks she'd worn to work today with her plain white blouse. Then she tossed the used paper towel in the trash and left the restroom.

Which was when she noticed someone new coming down the steps into the church basement.

A latecomer, was her initial thought.

Before she took a second look and recognized the man. Unless she was mistaken, that was Derek Camden.

She'd never met him. But not only had the Bronsons' dislike and resentment of the Camdens brought the well-known family to her attention whenever they were in the news or in magazine or newspaper articles, she also had some small knowledge of this specific Camden. He'd been involved for a brief time with her best friend Tyson's cousin—a woman Tyson referred to as the family nutcase—and Gia had seen a snapshot of the two together.

Being reasonably sure that was who he was, she moved to intercept him before he got out of the stairwell and could be seen by anyone else.

"Can I help you?" she asked in a hurry, hoping not to draw the attention of the Bronsons.

"Umm…I don't know. I heard through the grapevine that tonight was the night people were getting together to talk about helping Larry and Marion Bronson—that's the group I'm looking for…."

"But you're Derek Camden, aren't you?" Gia said.

"I am. And you are…?"

"Not going to let you in here."

His face erupted into a grin.

The face that she'd already noted was even more striking in person than it had been in the photograph. And he'd looked incredibly good in the photograph.

His hair was an even darker brown than hers was—verging on black—with just a touch of wave to the top that he left slightly longer than the short sides. His nose was the perfect length and shape—thin and straight. His mouth was just lush enough. He had the sexiest hint of a cleft in his chiseled chin. And nothing she'd heard about the Camden blue eyes had done his justice, because they were the vibrant blue of the delphiniums she loved to look out at through her kitchen window every morning.

And it all went with six foot two inches of muscular masculinity not at all hidden behind the tan slacks and cream-colored shirt he was wearing with his brown tie loosened at the open collar, and the suit coat he had hooked by a thumb over one impressively broad shoulder.

"You're not going to let me in here?" he repeated, as if her thinking she could stop him amused him no end.

"No, I'm not," Gia asserted. "It would ruin the Bronsons' night."

It only occurred to her as she said it that this man appeared to be about her own age and maybe didn't know what had been done by his family generations before. That maybe he was there purely in response to word getting out, and had genuinely just come to help. Without knowing that his family was at the heart of the Bronsons' hardship.

"I'm sorry, did you know that there's bad blood between the Bronsons and your family?" she asked.

The alarm in her tone only made him laugh. "A lot of people don't like the Camdens," was all he admitted to.

"This is more than just—" she wasn't sure how to put it so she repeated his words "—a lot of people not liking the Camdens on some sort of principal—"

"It's okay. I came to help anyway," he assured as if he didn't view an aversion to his family as an obstacle.

"Yeah…well…it wouldn't be okay with Larry and Marion, and I'm reasonably sure they wouldn't take help from any Camden," Gia said more bluntly because she was concerned that he wasn't getting the picture. "And this may not look like it, but it's a night out for them, they're having a good time talking to people they haven't seen in a while and I don't want it wrecked for them

She had no doubt the presence of a Camden would do just that.

"But I do want to help them," Derek Camden said.

He was kind of stubborn. Great looking and amiable and certainly nothing more than tickled by her blockade, but difficult to persuade.

"They lost their hotel years ago to H. J. Camden. So maybe if you give them the Camden store that was built where their hotel was…" Gia suggested to get her point across. And to test his response and possibly learn whether or not he knew the history.

It worked, because he flinched charmingly and Gia had the impression that he knew exactly what she was talking about. "I don't think I can do that. But that doesn't mean that I don't want to do *something.* And by the way, who *are* you?" he asked without any rancor.

"Gia Grant. I live next door to the Bronsons."

"And you've taken them under your wing," he guessed. "The guy who cuts my hair down on University had a donation jar. He said there was some *little lady* behind this. Is this whole thing your doing, Gia Grant?"

"We're friends *and* neighbors. The Bronsons are good, good people and I can't sit by and just watch what's happening to them—"

"Which is what, exactly?"

Gia glanced over her shoulder at the long lunch table where the group that was left was talking. They hadn't yet noticed that she wasn't back from the restroom, but that wasn't going to last forever.

"The longer I stand here, the more likely it is that neone is going to see you and, honestly, I won't let ut a damper on Larry and Marion's night."

 I *do* want to help," he insisted.

te, then."

He nodded that oh-so-handsome head sagely. "We're interested in more than just stuffing some cash in a donation jar. My grandmother isn't too much younger than the Bronsons, and let's say they've struck a chord with her. She sent me to represent the family and make sure whatever needs the Bronsons have are met."

"Then donate a *lot* of money. Anonymously, or they won't take it."

He inclined his head as if that might be a good solution but he just couldn't accept it. "We don't want to just throw some money at the problem. We want to find out what *all* of the problems are and lend a hand getting them addressed in the best way possible so these people can finish out their lives comfortably, safely and securely."

"You're admitting that what your family did way back when caused the problems, and now you have a responsibility to make things right," Gia surmised.

"We just want to help," he said, firmly holding that line and acknowledging nothing else.

Gia shook her head. "The Bronsons are in trouble. But they're proud people. I've convinced them to accept help from their friends and neighbors, their church, by assuring them that the help is coming from people they've given business to for decades, from the same people they've helped in the past or would help if the need arose even now and they could. I've promised them that it isn't charity, it's people who know and care about them just wanting to do something for them. But they hate you—I'm sorry to be so direct, but that's just a fact. I know them—they'll think that anything you do will have an ulterior motive. If they know you're behind a dime, they won't take it."

"Maybe you can persuade them to," he proposed.

"I don't know how I'd do that."

"I'll bet you can think of a way…" he said pointedly.

"You do owe them," Gia said matter-of-factly because it was true. And even though she knew how the Bronsons would feel about accepting anything from the Camdens, she also knew that they were in need of more help than what her efforts were producing. The Camdens' assistance could go much further in solving the elderly couple's problems.

"Maybe you could introduce me as a friend of yours and leave out the part about me being a Camden."

"They'd recognize you. They might not know exactly which Camden you are, but they follow your family like fans follow celebrities, begrudging you every step of the way. And they might be old, but mentally, they're both sharp as tacks. Nothing gets by them, and you wouldn't, either." With another glance over her shoulder to make sure no one was looking in this direction, Gia added, "And really, I want you to leave before they spot you."

"I'm not giving up," he said then, but he did step one step higher, which made him tower above Gia even more. "So how about I leave it to you to convince them to accept my help?"

He reached into his shirt pocket with his free hand and pulled out a business card. "All my numbers are on that."

Gia accepted the card.

"If I don't hear from you, you'll have me knocking on your door—don't forget you already told me that you live next to the Bronsons."

"I can't make any promises," Gia said, knowing full 'll that she had to do what she could to convince Larry Marion, because the Camdens—no matter how ble—still had the kind of resources the Bron-'ed.

"I'm relying on you anyway," he said, investing her with the responsibility despite her hedging.

"I'll do what I can if you just go!"

He grinned again and took another step up. "I'll tell you one thing," he said as he did, "you're the prettiest bouncer I've ever been ousted by."

"As if a Camden has ever been kicked out of any-place," Gia countered.

"You might be surprised."

"Just go!" she said, trying not to think that he was lingering in order to stare at her—which was how it appeared, because his beautiful blue eyes seemed to be taking in every inch of her and his expression said he was enjoying the view.

"Get back to me soon or I'll come for you..." he threatened in a way that didn't sound as if they were still talking about helping the Bronsons.

"No promises," Gia repeated firmly to let him know he wasn't wearing her down.

But he was. Just a tiny bit.

Enough so that, as she turned from the sight of him backing up the rest of the steps so he could go on study-ing her, she felt a smile come to the corners of her mouth.

Because although she had no idea why, just the way Derek Camden looked at her made her feel better about herself than the dinner invitation from the minister had.

Chapter Two

"Georgie! You feisty little beanbag, where are you?" Derek called when he went into his grandmother's house midmorning on Tuesday.

"She's in the greenhouse."

"Oh, hey, Jonah. Hey, Louie. I didn't see you guys up there."

Jonah Morrison—Derek's grandmother's old high school sweetheart and new husband since their wedding in June—seemed to be working on something on the stairs. Louie Haliburton—the male half of the married couple who had worked for the family as live-in staff for decades—was helping him.

"What's going on?" Derek asked the two older men.

"Fixing the banister," Louie answered.

"Or trying to," Jonah added.

"Need help?" Derek offered, even though he was in the midst of his workday and had only stopped by on his way back from a meeting with Camden Incorporated's bankers in his capacity as chief financial officer.

"Nah, we can handle it," Louie assured.

"I'll head for the greenhouse, then. Holler if you change your minds."

Derek went across the wide entryway, down the hallway that led straight to the kitchen. There he found Louie's wife, Margaret.

"Hey, Maggie-May," he greeted the stocky woman, who was old enough for retirement but was still on her hands and knees cleaning one of the ovens.

"Derek! Did we expect you today?"

He leaned over and kissed her rosy cheek. "Nope. Just stopped by to talk to Georgie."

"She's in the greenhouse."

"So I heard. That's where I'm headed."

"Staying for lunch?"

"Can't. Have to get back to the office. I only have a few minutes." He went through the kitchen to the greenhouse, where his grandmother was watering her prize orchids.

"Georgie…don't let me scare you…" he said in a mellow tone once he got there, because his grandmother's back was to him and he didn't want to startle the seventy-five-year-old.

Georgianna Camden was the matriarch of the Camden family, the woman who had raised all ten of her grandchildren after the plane crash that killed their parents and her husband. The rest of the family called her GiGi. Derek had always affectionately called her Georgie.

"As if I didn't hear you shouting from the doorway," his grandmother said, turning off the water.

He crossed the greenhouse to kiss her cheek, too, putting an arm around the shoulders that—like the rest of her—felt as cushy as a beanbag chair.

He gave her a little squeeze before letting her go. "I'm on my way back to the office, but I thought I'd stop for a few minutes to tell you that I went to that church your friend belongs to last night—"

"Jean didn't see you. I talked to her this morning."

"Checking up on me?" he asked with a laugh. "I went but I didn't get in. Some hot little number named Gia Grant caught me at the foot of the steps to the basement and wouldn't let me go any farther."

"I know that name—Jean can't say enough good things about her. She doesn't belong to their church, she's the Bronsons' neighbor and—"

"She's the one behind this deal to help the Bronsons—I know, the guy who cuts my hair told me. But last night she was also the guardian of the gate. Your friend Jean was right about the meeting to organize the work for the Bronsons, but what she didn't say was that the Bronsons themselves would be at the church. Gia Grant spotted me coming, recognized me somehow and wouldn't let me out of the stairwell. She said a Camden would ruin the Bronsons' night."

"Oh, dear…"

"Yeah. We might not have known about what went on between H.J. and those people until you read about it in the journals, but it isn't something they've forgotten."

The man who had started the Camden empire—Derek's great-grandfather H. J. Camden—had kept a journal while he was alive. Only recently rediscovered, it confirmed what H.J., his son, Hank, and his grandsons, Mitchum and Howard, had long been accused of—ruthless, unscrupulous business practices that trampled people and other businesses.

After reading the journals, Georgianna Camden and her grandchildren were determined to make amends for some of the worst of the wrongs done. Including what had been done to the Bronsons.

"Gia Grant says that no matter how much trouble the Bronsons are in," Derek informed his grandmother, "they have too much pride to take anything from us. Her recommendation was that we just donate money anonymously.... And the anonymity wouldn't be so bad for us, because then we'd be avoiding any admission of guilt...."

GiGi shook her head at that suggestion. "I know we need to keep from making any kind of open, public acknowledgment of wrongdoing so we don't have people coming out of the woodwork to sue us for things the Camdens didn't do—"

"Big corporations and money make for easy targets," Derek confirmed. "And you know there are stories out there accusing us of stuff that *didn't* happen—so, yeah, if we say some of the accusations are well founded, there'll be an avalanche of see-I-told-you-so lawsuits for *un*-founded complaints that will tie us up in court until hell freezes over."

"We also don't want to come out and say that H.J. and your grandfather, father and uncle really were involved in underhanded business practices—there's family loyalty at stake here, too," GiGi said under her breath, because this was something that she didn't discuss if Jonah, Margaret or Louie were around.

"So a payout would be a whole lot easier, but it wouldn't protect us," Derek acknowledged.

"And we wouldn't necessarily achieve our goal of making amends with a simple payout," GiGi added. "In this case in particular, just donating some money might not be the best answer for the Bronsons. Jean says they have no family. No one beyond that Gia girl—and she's only a neighbor—to look after them or help them. They're in their eighties, so there are some health problems, and Jean isn't sure they should be living on their own anymore. And what if one of them dies and the other is left all alone—?"

"You want to just move them in here?" Derek joked.

"You know how I feel about this one, Derek. It's going to need some involvement on our part for what remains of the Bronsons' lives," GiGi insisted. "And you know that just donating money doesn't guarantee that the money will get into the right hands or get used in the ways it should be used, especially down the road. We have to know that these people have whatever they need to finish out their lives—financially and otherwise. And their needs can change depending on how their health or situation changes. We have to have some kind of presence in their lives. So you have to make nice with them. Win them over and establish a relationship with them so we can help later on, too, if need be. For their sake."

"I touched on some of that with Gia. But I still couldn't even get in the door...."

"Well, you're going to have to do whatever it takes to accomplish that, honey. Maybe first you'll have to win over the guard at the gate...."

That brought a vivid image of Gia Grant to mind—something that had been happening at the drop of a hat since he'd met her last night.

Maybe because of that hair, he thought.

That hair was just great!

Every time the memory of it popped into his head it made him smile.

Full and thick and shiny and wildly curly...

That was probably why it appealed to him. He liked things that were a little on the wild side.

And he'd loved that hair....

Plus, she had big, beautiful brown eyes the color of espresso sprinkled with gold dust.

And peaches-and-cream skin that didn't show a single flaw.

And a straight nose that turned up almost imperceptibly and just a little impudently at the end.

And a picture-perfect mouth that was exactly the kind he liked to kiss because her lips were slightly full and sumptuous-looking....

All on top of a body that was tight but still soft and curvaceous even if she wasn't particularly tall....

Oh, yeah, he'd done a *lot* of thinking about Gia Grant since last night....

For no reason he could put his finger on.

"I did ask her to intervene on my behalf, but she wasn't too optimistic that she could convince the Bronsons to accept anything from us," he told his grandmother when he'd pulled himself out of his thoughts of Gia.

"Like I said, win her over first, then," GiGi advised. "The better she likes you, the more apt she is to sell you to the Bronsons. And from what I understand from Jean, that shouldn't be too painful for you—Jean says she's never met a nicer, friendlier, more helpful person, and that she's beautiful to boot and doesn't even seem to know it. So she's humble, too. I know Jean has her eye on her for Lucas once his divorce is final, and she and the other ladies in her church committees are all worried that their pastor is very taken with this Gia Grant—"

"So wouldn't that make her perfect for their pastor—a paragon of virtue like that?"

"Shame on you for saying that like it's a bad thing! That's what gets you into trouble."

No truer words were ever spoken, so Derek couldn't deny it. Besides, he didn't dare. Not after his most recent blunder, the one that had really caused him to cross the line.

The one he wanted to kick himself over.

The one that had cost him a bundle and most of his dignity....

"If she's all that your friend says she is, why wouldn't the church ladies *want* her for their pastor?" he asked more respectfully.

"She's divorced."

"And that's an issue?"

"It's only an issue when it comes to their minister— they want someone purer for him, I guess. Plus, like I said, Jean wants Gia for Lucas—"

"Lucas Paulie is a weasel," Derek said, not understanding why it rubbed him wrong to think of the woman he'd spent all of about five minutes with either the church pastor he didn't know or the guy he did know.

"I didn't realize you disliked Lucas Paulie so much," GiGi said.

"I just wouldn't wish him on some poor unsuspecting do-gooder."

"There it is again, Derek James Camden! *Do-gooder*—that is *not* a bad thing. A nice girl is what you need. You'd better start looking for one and stay away from what you've been bringing around here since you were a teenager. Haven't you learned your lesson *yet?*"

"I have, Georgie," he said on a sigh. "I just can't help it if the...*tame* ones don't do it for me. I like a little spice."

"What you've brought around here is not a *little spice*. And this last one—"

"I know. You don't have to tell me—again—how damn stupid that was."

"And yet here you are, barely out from under the mess you were in, looking down your nose at someone doing some good."

"I'm not looking down my nose at Gia Grant."

He was doing anything but that, if the truth be known. He sure as hell hadn't been thinking bad things about her since last night.

It just didn't matter. He knew the way things went for him—regardless of how beautiful the woman, regardless of how much he might respect and admire her or what she was doing, in no time the good girls just couldn't keep his interest. In no time they started to seem ordinary. They started to get predictable. They started to bore him to tears.

But he wasn't a kid anymore. And he had no business letting himself be sucked into situations with the bad girls anymore.

It had been bad enough when he *was* a kid, but now it was inexcusable. Especially when it embarrassed the whole family right along with himself. Like this last time.

Which was why he was lying low. Why he was doing some self-imposed penance by staying away from all women for a while. Why he was putting his energies into work and the Camden Foundation and trying to make things up to the Bronsons the way his grandmother had asked him to. Even if he was reasonably sure that his grandmother's intent was to keep him well-occupied so he wouldn't have time to get involved with anyone else for a while.

Not that he could blame her....

"I gave Gia Grant my card and told her if I didn't

hear from her I'd track her down," Derek said then, ignoring how much he was looking forward to seeing her again. "She apparently lives next door to the Bronsons, so even if I have to knock on the wrong door before I get the right one, I'll find her. Then maybe I can try to go through her to get to the Bronsons. I think she may have seen the benefit of our help over her donation jars and church volunteers, but whether or not she can convince the Bronsons—"

"You'll find a way in," Georgianna said.

"I really will, Georgie. I'm not going to let you—or any of the rest of the family—down again."

"I hope not," GiGi said. "Maybe you should try to let this Grant girl be a good influence on you for a change...."

"You never know," he said, rather than defend himself the way he might have done before the latest fiasco. "But for now I'd better get back to the office."

GiGi nodded. As she reached to turn the water on again, she said, "You're a good boy, Derek. I don't know why you have such a soft spot for bad girls. Maybe you can turn over a new leaf."

"Tryin', Georgie, I'm tryin'."

But even as Gia Grant's oh-so-lovely face came to mind again, he wondered if he could.

"A chicken and steaks and a roast, Gia? You could freeze these, you know," Marion lectured.

"I already froze a bunch. It's cheaper to buy at the bulk warehouse, but I end up with more than I can use. You're helping me out by taking some of it." It was the same thing Gia said every time she brought Larry and Marion groceries. Their budget was so strapped that meat had become a luxury item. But pride wouldn't allow them to let Gia provide that for them unless she made it sound as if they were doing her a favor. So that was the slant she put on it.

"Well, thank you. You're too good to us," Marion said as she put away the groceries that included some other things Gia knew they liked but couldn't afford for themselves.

"Let's open one of those beers right now," Larry suggested.

Marion obliged her husband and opened the cupboard to get glasses. "Will you have some of this, Gia?"

"No, you guys go ahead," she said. She declined their offers every time, too.

"I know you didn't buy *this* for yourself," Marion said as she poured the beer into two glasses.

Gia laughed. "And *I* know how much you and Larry like your little swig of beer before dinner," she said, using the term they used.

They were in the Bronsons' kitchen late Tuesday afternoon. Gia had left work at three o'clock, done some shopping and was now delivering groceries as a pretext for what she really came to talk to the Bronsons about.

The couple had been in such good spirits when they'd left the church the night before that Gia hadn't wanted to dampen them by bringing up Derek Camden. But he'd somehow gotten her cell phone number and left a message this afternoon about the status of persuading Larry and Marion to let him help them.

Gia hadn't returned his call yet, but his invitation to meet her for coffee at seven to talk had inspired this visit.

And given the boring evening she was facing a whole new spin....

Not that she was eager to see Derek Camden again, she told herself. Even if he had shadowed her thoughts since she'd first set eyes on him last night. It was just that she didn't have anything else to do tonight and hopefully the evening would end up benefitting Larry and Marion.

When they were all seated around the Bronsons' aged, scarred kitchen table, Gia said, "There's something I want to talk to you guys about. You didn't know it last night, but a Camden showed up at the church—Derek Camden...."

Marion looked alarmed. Larry was instantly angry.

"What're they doing, coming for the money you've raised to help us?" Larry said.

"Didn't they get enough when they took everything from us? Are those richy-riches even after our pennies now?" Marion said, her tone harsh.

This was the reason Gia hadn't wanted Derek Camden to crash last night's get-together.

"There's no way they could get hold of what's been donated—that's in a secure account at the bank under your names and mine," Gia assured them. Then she added cautiously, "Derek Camden said he came to help... I'm not sure how—"

"Some way that'll put more in his pocket!" Larry again.

"They're probably looking to take our house now!" Marion said, sounding genuinely afraid. "Like with the hotel—right when we were struggling to keep it, they swooped in and made it so we couldn't. Now when the bank wants the house, they're coming for that, too!"

"No, no, no," Gia said quickly, trying to calm the elderly woman's fears. "I'm sure they don't want your house—"

"They probably want the whole block. The whole area for another one of their damn stores!" Larry said, getting more and more worked up. "You'd better watch out, Gia, they could be coming for your place, too!"

"They already have two stores nearby—the one that was built where your hotel was, and the one on Colorado Boulevard. And we're zoned residential—"

"They pay off people to change zoning—don't be fooled by that," Larry contended.

Gia had known this was not going to be easy. "Okay, I know how you both feel about the Camdens—and with good reason—"

"You bet we have reason—they robbed us," Larry ranted.

"I know—"

"Dirty crooks!" This from Marion.

"But what was done to you two was a long time ago, by H. J. Camden. And I'm not defending what he did—" Gia said quickly, because she could see that more comments were coming from the elderly couple "—but H. J. Camden is long gone and maybe—just maybe— the Camdens in charge now want to make up for what H. J. Camden did...."

"Did they say that? Did they admit what he did? Because we couldn't prove anything, but if they confessed, maybe we can sue their pants off now!" Larry sounded excited by the prospect.

"He didn't admit anything," Gia said. "Derek Camden only claimed that he wanted to help."

"How could we ever sue them even if they confessed?" Marion reasoned with her husband. "We'd still be going up against a million of their lawyers. And with what? Where would we even find a lawyer to take them on? Or hire one with no money? They'd crush us like bugs—again!"

"But the three of us know that they still owe you," Gia

said, hoping to ride the wave of Marion's logic. "Derek Camden said they want to help financially, but that they also want to make sure you guys are taken care of all the way around. And we could use help like that…."

"Not from Camdens we couldn't!" Larry proclaimed.

"We could, though," Gia said gently. "We've raised a few thousand dollars and we have people coming over to help clean up the yard and paint the house, but a few thousand dollars isn't going to keep the bank from foreclosing for long—the best it will do is pay some of the back payments and stall so we can sell the house after it's been fixed up."

Gia hated—*hated*—when she had to remind them of the cold, hard facts, because it just deflated them both and made them look as old as they were. Both were white haired—Larry only had a wreath of hair around a mostly bald head, and Marion wore hers in a short style she cut herself. There wasn't an ounce of fat or much muscle left on Larry's five-foot-eight frame, and Marion could easily qualify as frail—she was barely five feet tall and didn't weigh a hundred pounds. They both had blue eyes that still showed a zest for life, and ordinarily they both stood straight and moved fairly spryly. But whenever they discussed their current predicament, it just sucked the life out of them right before Gia's eyes.

"You know I'm with you if that's the best we can do," she added to reassure them. "My basement apartment is yours and I'd love to have you with me. But I know that neither one of you *wants* to do that. You want to stay in this house. And with the kind of money the Camdens have…" She shrugged. "Not that Derek Camden made any promises, but if there's any chance left of coming up with enough to maybe keep you here…"

"I still think they have something up their sleeve," Larry grumbled.

"You can't trust them," Marion concurred.

And they both sounded so beaten that it broke Gia's heart.

But as much as she wanted to side with them and tell them she would throw whatever Derek Camden offered back in his face on their behalf, she had to look out for what was best for them. And if the Camdens followed through on their promise, it could mean better than what she'd been able to accomplish.

"I'll do anything you want. This is completely up to you," she told them, in hopes of making them feel as if they had some control, some power, some choice in the matter. "But if you'll accept help from the Camdens, I'll make sure there are no strings attached to anything they give. That there's nothing up their sleeve. That nothing about this can hurt you—"

"Or you," Marion contributed.

"Or me—in any way. And if you never want to set eyes on Derek Camden or any other Camden—"

"Get him over here to pull weeds and let me turn the hose on him," Larry muttered.

"You can't turn the hose on someone like that," Marion chastised. "He'd probably sue *us!*"

"I can turn my hose on anybody I want to turn my hose on," Larry contended cantankerously.

"We could bring him lemonade while he works and lace it with laxative—then he'd never know what hit him!" Marion suggested, making Gia laugh.

"So you want me to get him over here to help work so you can have a little payback?" Gia asked, reasonably sure that they wouldn't actually do either of the things they were threatening.

"A Camden working for us…" Marion mused.

"That'd serve them right," Larry added.

Gia could tell that they were both finding some fuel in their retribution plots, and she was glad to see them rally.

"So you'll let me talk to Derek Camden about what they're offering? And you aren't opposed to having him come over here and do some of the work?" she said, since she thought she should strike while the iron was hot.

"We don't want anything to do with them," Larry reiterated.

"No, we don't," Marion confirmed. "But you can take whatever they're offering, Gia," she said, as if anything coming from the Camdens through her made it more palatable. "As long as you watch them like a hawk— because they *do* owe us, and whatever helps you help us we'll take."

"But don't say anything that lets them off the hook for anything, those lousy shysters!" Larry added.

Gia marveled at a phenomenon she'd witnessed before—sometimes it was as if they'd communicated with each other and come to a decision without ever having talked about it. Apparently seventy years of marriage put them on the same wavelength somehow. Or maybe they'd always been on the same wavelength and that was why they'd been able to stay married for so long.

But regardless of how they'd come to this particular conclusion, Gia was just glad they had.

"Then I'll tell Derek Camden that we'll take his help."

The scowl on Larry's face and the dour, forlorn creases on Marion's brow told her how unwillingly the offer was being accepted. But Gia thought it was better to get out before they changed their minds. Besides, it would give the Bronsons some time alone to rant and rail about it to their hearts' content while she went off to deal with Derek Camden.

And why she felt as excited as a teenager who had just finagled permission from her parents to see someone forbidden—who she really, really wanted to see again—Gia didn't quite understand.

She was a long way from being a teenager.

Larry and Marion weren't her parents.

And Derek Camden was forbidden because Gia was forbidding herself from him.

Because even if she was ready to date, she wouldn't date a man like Derek Camden. She might not have a grudge against the Camdens the way Larry and Marion did, but her own past experience taught her to avoid men like Derek.

Her ex-husband was also a man with deep-rooted loyalties to a big, corrupt, ruthless, unprincipled clan-like family, and that was a hot-button issue for her.

So Derek Camden was not someone she would even consider getting involved with.

Personally anyway.

For Larry and Marion's sake, she would have contact with him—and she *would* watch him like a hawk, as Marion had ordered—but that was the beginning and end of it.

So any sort of excitement at the thought of seeing him again was something to squash hard and fast.

Which she did as she said goodbye to the Bronsons and left them sitting at the table.

And yet on her way home, a tiny blip of excitement still registered when she started to consider what she was going to wear to see him tonight....

When Gia returned Derek Camden's call, he asked if they could meet at a Cherry Creek bakery rather than the coffee shop he'd suggested in his message.

It didn't matter to Gia where they met, so she agreed. Then she fixed herself a sandwich for dinner and decided she couldn't wear anything different for this meeting than what she had on.

Not that she didn't want to change out of the brown slacks and tan pin-tucked blouse she'd worn to work. She just couldn't let herself. This wasn't a date and she needed not to forget that.

But she told herself that it was purely for her own comfort that she unleashed her hair from the ponytail it had been in all day, brushed it out and let it fall loose and full into its naturally curly mass.

And when it came to refreshing her blush and adding a neutral eye shadow, some eyeliner and more mascara, it was merely to look at the top of her game in order to warn him that he'd better not try to put one over on her.

Arriving at the bakery five minutes early, she spotted Derek Camden through the storefront windows as she pulled her sedan into a parking spot.

He was also still in work clothes, although he'd taken off his tie and suit jacket. He was wearing gray-blue suit pants and a pale blue dress shirt, and Gia's first thought was that no one should look that good after a full day.

But there was just the hint of scruff to his sculpted jawline, and his dark hair was the ideal amount of disheveled; combined with the perfectly tailored shirt and pants, it formed a very sexy contrast.

A split second after the thought occurred to Gia, she reprimanded herself for it.

Handsome and sexy did not make the man. Handsome and sexy could, however, provide camouflage for something very ugly under the surface or behind the scenes.

It was a fact of life that she'd learned well and wouldn't let herself forget.

It would have been easy to, though, because when she went into the bakery and Derek noticed her, he smiled a smile that said he liked what he saw. And it made her heart beat a little faster.

"Hi, thanks for coming," he greeted her.

"Hi," Gia responded simply.

"Excuse me just a minute."

For a moment his attention turned back to the woman behind the counter. "So I can pick up the cake tomorrow at one—that's great, just what I need." Then, with a nod toward Gia, he said, "Let me add what we have now to the tab and I'll settle up with you later?"

When the woman agreed, he said to Gia, "I don't know if you've been here before, but you can't go wrong with anything—"

"Lava cake, Bea," Gia said to the woman, who was already taking one from the case and putting it on a plate.

"Heated with an extra dollop of hot fudge on top," the woman recited her order from memory.

Derek laughed. "Ah, I see I'm not introducing you to anything new."

"She's our favorite chocoholic," the owner of the bakery informed him.

He ordered lemon-meringue pie, and they both asked for iced tea. Then, while the shop owner got everything ready, Derek led Gia to one of the small café tables.

"We order all of our office celebration cakes here," he explained. "Tomorrow I'm surprising my assistant with a little engagement party."

A head-honcho Camden was ordering the cake himself? Her ex-husband and the rest of his family would never have bothered.

"How about you? How do you know this place?" he asked.

"I work around the corner and come at least once a day."

Derek Camden's well-shaped eyebrows rose. "Every day?" he said, taking a quick glance at her body as if wondering where the calories went.

"Sometimes it's the only thing I eat all day," she confessed.

"Chocolate every time?"

Her shrug confirmed it.

He laughed. "You *are* a chocoholic."

Gia didn't deny it.

"What do you do around the corner?"

"I'm a botanist. I work for a company that makes herbal supplements and medicines."

The eyebrows went up again. "Really?"

"My ex said I'm just a glorified gardener."

"Well, I'm just an accountant, so it sounds more impressive than that."

He was being humble. Gia knew he was the chief financial officer of Camden Incorporated. But she preferred humility to arrogance. Elliot had been all arrogance.

Not that she *preferred* Derek Camden, she amended in her thoughts. The only way she wanted to compare him with her ex was in terms of their similarities—like the fact that they both came from big, powerful, rich families willing to do dishonest, shifty, devious and deceitful things.

"How did you get my cell phone number?" she asked then, continuing the vein of small talk while they waited for their desserts.

"My grandmother is friends with Jean Paulie—I believe she was one of the church members at your meeting last night—"

"She was."

"Jean is one of the people who brought the Bronsons to our attention—her and the guy who cuts my hair because he had a donation jar in his shop. Anyway, I asked my grandmother if Jean had your number and she did."

Gia nodded.

"My turn—how did you know who I was last night?" he asked.

"My best friend is Tyson Biggs. You dated his cousin and I saw a picture of you with her." Gia didn't add that the image had stuck with her because he was so terrific looking. Or that now that she'd seen him in person she couldn't shake his image from her mind at all....

He grinned. "Sharon. Dragon nails, always in stilettos, carried a purse that was also a fish tank—complete with her goldfish in it—claimed to be psychic..."

"That would be Sharon," Gia confirmed.

He smiled conspiratorially, in a way that was much too engaging. "Did she ever get a *reading* for you right?"

"I've never had her do one of her actual *readings*. She's offered, but on the two times I've met her she told me out of the blue—"

"To prove her *powers*—she likes to do that," he said as if it amused him.

"Well, the first time she told me I was pregnant and I wasn't. The second time she said to watch out because I was going to lose my job. Luckily, that didn't happen, either."

"Yeah, she's never gotten anything right that I know of. She isn't even good at guessing," he concluded with a laugh that wasn't at all disparaging or unkind. "I haven't seen Sharon in...I'm not even sure how long."

"So long that you've had time to get married and settle down?" she asked because she was curious. She'd heard about Sharon and about her friends that he'd dated later—also all wackjobs, according to Tyson. But Gia didn't know anything about Derek Camden beyond that, and she reasoned that if he'd married and settled down he might be more trustworthy in the Bronsons' eyes.

But the question that shouldn't have been difficult to answer instead seemed to puzzle him.

"Huh…" he said, rubbing the back of his neck and suddenly making a face that conveyed discomfort and confusion. "I was going to jump in and say no, never married. But then I remembered that that isn't exactly true anymore. Is annulled a marital status?"

"Annulled… I don't know, I've never met anyone who was annulled."

"Yeah, me, neither…" he said with a frown.

Their desserts arrived and when the shop owner left them to eat he didn't explain further, leaving Gia curious but not feeling free to ask more than she already had.

Then he changed the subject and she really couldn't indulge her curiosity.

"So did you talk to the Bronsons about accepting some help from us?"

"I did."

He smiled at her tone. "It didn't go well?"

"It went the way I thought it would. But they did come around. They said they would let you help me help them."

He nodded slowly as he ate a bite of his pie. "Okay. A little convoluted but still something. And I'll take what I can get at this point. So what do you have planned?"

Gia had taken a bite of her own dessert as he said that. And when it came to chocolate, there was no rushing her. So she held up a finger in front of her mouth to signify a pause as she savored the warm, rich, dark chocolate of her lava cake.

He smiled. "No hurry, enjoy yourself."

"The lemon pie is good, but next time try one of these," she advised when her mouth wasn't full. "It's just the right blend of chocolates and just melty enough and just…amazing."

His smile stretched into a grin. "Not a big chocolate guy so I'll take your word for it."

If anything could turn her off, it should be that!

But somehow it didn't make him look any less appealing to her, so she just filed the information away and answered his inquiry into what she had planned to help the Bronsons.

"There's a day of yard work and a day of home repairs to get their place in better shape," she said. "And I'm cleaning out their stuff and collecting things to sell at a yard sale that I'm hoping will also raise some money— if you want to bring anything for that, do it. This coming Saturday is the yard work, the Saturday after that will be the home repair day and the Saturday after that is the yard sale."

"So yard work and home repairs—they haven't been able to keep their place up," he deduced.

"They haven't had the money, and they're just getting too old to do most things—"

"Should they be moved into a retirement home or assisted living?"

It was a perfectly reasonably suggestion, one she and Tyson had swatted back and forth, one she'd thrown out to the Bronsons.

And yet hearing it from Derek Camden made her recall Larry and Marion's concern that the Camdens were after their house.

Which still didn't seem at all likely to Gia.

But even though there wasn't anything intimidating about Derek Camden—in fact, he seemed down-to-earth, open and friendly—she'd also heard so much from the Bronsons about the evil Camdens that she felt some concern herself.

"Retirement homes and assisted living are expensive, too, and the Bronsons are really against going somewhere with *old people*—"

He laughed again. "They're how old themselves?"

"Eighty-nine and eighty-seven," Gia said with a hint of humor at the irony of that. "But staying together in their house is a big deal to them."

"Okay. So beyond their home needing some work inside and out, what else is going on with them?"

He'd said the night before that he wanted to get the full picture, not to merely give money but to make sure the Bronsons had what they needed all the way around. So logically, what he was asking was just a way to get that full picture.

But still, Gia was a little uncomfortable giving this man too many details that would let him know exactly how vulnerable the couple was.

"A lot of things are going on with them," she said ambiguously, opting only to give him an overview. "They live on a *very* limited budget. Costs for everything are always rising. They aren't in bad health for their ages but there are some issues—they both have high blood pressure and some heart things, some arthritis, Marion has osteoporosis. And every time they go to a doctor there's another medication added—"

"Not your herbal supplements and medicines?"

"I can't really recommend any of those because they take so many prescription meds I'm afraid of interfering with something or giving them a supplement that reacts badly with a prescription drug—so no. But I help them pay their bills and balance their checkbook—because they both have trouble holding a pen and seeing small print—and there are months when I can't believe the cost of their prescriptions."

"Do they need better insurance? A cheaper place to get their prescriptions filled?"

"I've looked into both of those things and done the best I can for them, but the bottom line is that some things fall outside of their coverage and there's nothing that can be done about it."

"Except to get them more money to pay the expenses they have."

Gia conceded with a shrug and hoped she hadn't said too much.

"So where do I start to help you help them?" he asked as he finished his pie.

Gia couldn't risk telling him too much about the Bronsons' predicament until she was sure his motives really were pure. But the only way she could think to get a better feel for him was to get to know him a little and see if he seemed trustworthy. And she didn't know how else to do that except to enlist him in the manual-labor portions of what was going on and spend some time with him. Talking to him. Watching him.

Even if it meant tempting Larry to turn the hose on him or Marion to lace lemonade with laxatives....

So, in response to his query about where he should start to help, she said, "Like I said, Saturday we're starting with the yard and we can always use two more hands...."

"Okay," he said without skipping a beat. "Are the Bronsons going to throw rocks at me if I show up on their doorstep, though?"

Maybe *he* was psychic....

"I hope not," was the best Gia could promise. "Their bark tends to be worse than their bite—"

"At eighty-seven and eighty-nine their teeth probably aren't their own."

"Every one of Marion's is and she's very proud of them," Gia corrected his joke. "But I'll run with the you-helping-me-to-help-them angle and I think you'll be safe." She didn't add that the Bronsons liked the idea of a Camden working for them, so they were apt to gloat about it—whether to his face or not she couldn't be sure.

"Then just tell me when and where to show up and I'll be there," he said.

Gia gave him the details and finished her lava cake. There didn't seem to be any more to discuss at this juncture, so she offered to pay for her own dessert as a signal that the meeting had come to a conclusion.

"It's going on the tab," he reminded her, refusing to even allow her to leave a tip.

He stood up when she did, and Gia tried not to be bowled over by the pure magnitude of the man as she slipped the strap of her purse over her shoulder, thinking that talking to him so far had not been a hardship, and watching him work on Saturday likely wouldn't be, either....

"Thank you for playing go-between," he said then.

"I'm just looking out for Larry and Marion," she countered.

"They're lucky to have you."

"I'm the lucky one—I don't have any family and they've become that for me."

He nodded as if he understood something about that, although she had no idea what and he didn't offer an explanation.

Instead he said, "I guess I'll see you Saturday, then."

"I'll supply the gloves," she added as they said good-bye and she left him to deal with the bill for their desserts and his office cake.

Then she returned to her car, studying him through the plate-glass windows again as she did and counting how many days would have to pass before Saturday came.

So many...

Oh, no—I don't have any reason to think that! she silently shouted at herself when she realized that was what had actually gone through her mind.

And to punish herself, she spent the short drive home recalling what it had been like to be married to a man who could well be Derek Camden's counterpart.

Chapter Three

"So you don't think there's any way he's going to show up," Gia said to Tyson Biggs on Saturday morning as they had a cup of coffee before going next door to begin the yard work on the Bronsons' property.

Gia's tall, lanky blond friend repeated his prediction, a frown on his hawkish face. "Derek Camden? No way."

Gia and Tyson had been best friends since childhood. His family had lived in the house directly behind her grandparents' house, where she'd grown up.

Gia had received the two-story house where she now lived in the divorce settlement—it was formerly one of her ex-husband's rental properties. Gia lived on the ground floor, but the second floor had been turned into an apartment, where Tyson was living while his own house was being built, and the basement apartment was vacant, so she could potentially use it for Larry and Marion.

"You don't really think Derek Camden is coming here to do yard work, do you?" Tyson asked.

The answer to that was yes, she had thought that. Until now. In fact, Derek Camden was pretty much all she'd thought about since Tuesday night, with the prospect of him coming today the light at the end of the tunnel.

Not that she'd wanted to admit that. But denying it didn't keep Tyson's skepticism from knocking the wind out of her sails just the same.

"What was it your ex liked to say? He could *say* anything, that didn't mean he had to do it," Tyson reminded her.

Gia nodded. "He did like to say that. With that smug smile he had when he felt like he was outsmarting someone by telling them what they wanted to hear when he didn't have any intention of making good on it. But Derek Camden claims he really wants to help."

"People like the Camdens pay people to do *their* yard work, G, they don't turn around and do other people's yard work themselves."

That did make sense.

"You met him, right?" she asked then, wondering if she had been completely mistaken in believing that he truly was determined to help the Bronsons. After all, she'd been totally misled by her ex-husband, so her track record was hardly reliable.

"I only met him that once when he was dating Sharon. But it was in a loud, crowded club—I just ran into them, had one drink and left."

"But you said he was nice to you and you didn't know what a guy like him was doing with Sharon."

"Right, I remember. And it's true—he wasn't her usual type. He seemed normal. But he was with her—so how normal could he be? Plus, Elliot was always nice, too—I'm not sure that means much with these guys. I think they just learn good social graces early to help cover up their darker side. Or maybe as a distraction so you don't see the knife in the back coming."

That had been true of Elliot.

"Well, if Derek Camden only gives a check, that'll still be something," Gia said. "The work is getting done with or without him."

"But why do you sound disappointed—were you really counting on him for some reason today?"

"Me? No! I have you and people from work and a couple of friends from the Botanical Gardens and some neighbors and the pastor and a whole group from the Bronsons' church coming. We'll be able to get it all done."

"Yeah, I can't imagine that a Camden used to living in the lap of luxury would be much help anyway." But then Tyson narrowed his hazel eyes at her. "You don't *like* this guy, do you?"

"I haven't found anything to *dis*like," Gia said with a negligent shrug. "At least not about him personally, if you take away what his family did to Larry and Marion. But no, I don't *like* him, either. I don't even know him."

She really only knew the way he looked. Her ex-husband had been good-looking, too—not as good-looking as Derek Camden, but still, no slouch. As time had gone on and she'd looked deeper, though, she'd begun to think "handsome is as handsome does," and those good looks had meant less and less to her.

"But it's enough to know what Derek Camden comes from," Tyson said, as if he needed to open her eyes. "The Camdens could buy and sell the Grants a thousand times over, and their reputation is even worse—sneakier, but worse. Getting involved with a Camden after just getting away from the Grants would be like going from the frying pan into the fire."

"Oh, I know," Gia agreed wholeheartedly. "Even the hint of shadiness means I don't want anything to do with them."

"Plus, what Sharon didn't like about him was the whole family connection. There's a ton of them and they're all joined at the hip—they work together, they hang out together, there's a family dinner at the grandmother's house every Sunday that none of them ever miss—"

"And believe me, no one knows better than I do that in a family that tight there's no real room for other people. Even spouses are always outsiders." Gia knew that from her own experience; it was something she and Tyson had talked about numerous times before.

"But none of this matters," she said to her friend when she realized they were just rehashing. "I'm not ready to even date right now—I told you I just turned down dinner with the church pastor, and who's more upstanding than him? And even if I was back on the market, people like the Camdens are everything I spent three years fighting tooth and nail to get away from—I would never get into anything like that again."

"And let's also not forget that Derek Camden dated my crazy cousin Sharon," Tyson added in support of Gia. "Plus, she must be the type he goes for because he dated two of her whacko friends after the breakup. I doubt that you're off-the-wall enough for that guy—unless you want to cut your hair into a spiky Mohawk and dye it blue...."

"This hair in a Mohawk?" Gia said with a laugh, pulling a springy curl from her ponytail.

"And I'm good, but I don't think I could face another

divorce from one of those people," Tyson added as if to seal the anti–Derek Camden deal.

Tyson was rated one of Denver's top-five divorce attorneys and had represented Gia when she'd divorced Elliot Grant. But the Grants' dirty fighting and false accusations against Tyson himself had prompted an inquiry from the Bar Association. It had all taken its toll on him and his practice, and wasn't something Gia wanted to put him through again.

"Don't worry, never again, Ty," Gia assured him. "When I'm ready to get back out there, it will only be with nice, average guys from nice, average families."

Gia poured what remained of her coffee down the sink and rinsed her cup, then took Tyson's to do the same so they could get next door to work.

Where Derek Camden probably would *not* show up because Tyson was right.

And where she would throw herself into the job and try not to feel as if she'd wasted almost an entire week fantasizing about Derek Camden flexing muscles to hoist fertilizer bags and paving stones....

Tyson was wrong.

Derek Camden arrived at the Bronsons' small red-brick two-bedroom house along with everyone else enlisted to work on Saturday. He wasn't even a minute late.

His outfit for the occasion—tennis shoes, old jeans and a plain green crewneck T-shirt—let Gia know she hadn't imagined the muscles behind those dress shirts the two times she'd seen him before. The well-worn, unflashy clothes also caused him to fit in seamlessly with the other volunteers.

And when she introduced him to the group, he cut her

off before she said his last name and was simply *Derek* to everyone except her and Tyson.

Derek mentioned how he and Tyson had met the one time, even remembering that Tyson was an attorney and a diehard Miami Hurricanes football fan. He also asked about Tyson's cousin Sharon, wishing her well without any sign of bitterness in regards to their relationship that hadn't panned out.

Then he pitched in. Not only did he have a can-do attitude, he had a surprising amount of knowledge and experience to back it up, especially when he offered to mow the lawn and actually repaired the lawnmower to do it.

But Gia's conversation with Tyson before leaving home served as a warning to her not to be too impressed.

Sure, Derek Camden could fix a lawnmower and mow the lawn.

Sure, he could hoist fertilizer bags and paving stones with the best of them—flexing muscles that made Gia's mouth water in a way that didn't happen at the sight of anyone else's flexing muscles.

Sure, he couldn't have been more pleasant or agreeable or uncomplaining.

Sure, he made friends with everyone there and she even watched Tyson accept more and more of his overtures as the day went on.

But she continued to remind herself that appearances could be deceiving, and that she would not—*could* not—let herself be deceived by them.

Which wasn't always easy to remember as the day went on and she got an eyeful of broad shoulders, thick thighs and a tight, perfectly shaped derriere she knew she had no business looking at.

And yet somehow couldn't help stealing a glimpse of over and over again....

* * *

By six o'clock the Bronsons' front and back yards were in better shape than they'd been in since Gia had known the elderly couple. Weeds were gone, bushes and trees were trimmed and the lawn was a well-manicured green carpet.

The volunteers had added a sandstone path from the front to the back and a second path from the back patio out to the toolshed. Landscapers had built a multitiered rock garden with room for flowers to be planted in the spring, and two of the horticulturists had planted shrubbery to line the fence in back. Gia and another botanist had formed a perennial garden just below the front porch on each side of the steps leading to the house.

The final effect was a vast improvement and upgrade that would require only minimal, easy maintenance either for Gia or for any new owner should the house have to be sold.

Throughout the day Larry had been in the center of things, unable to work but chatting with the people who were, while Marion went in and out of the house with beverages and cookies.

Gia had kept an eye on them both and had seen no indication that they were going to turn the hose on Derek or secretly dose him with laxatives, and she was glad that really had only been a joke.

But after both Larry and Marion had had Gia confirm on the sly that Derek was who they thought he was, neither of the Bronsons ventured too near to him, either. Or made any effort to talk to him the way they did everyone else.

For Derek's part, he gave them the space they so obviously wanted, and the one time there was unavoidable contact he was polite and respectfully pleasant without pushing anything or going overboard trying to win their favor.

It was the best way he could have handled it, but still Gia wasn't exactly sure what was going to happen when the work was finished and everyone—including Tyson—left, and only Derek and Gia remained to roll up hoses and put away tools.

As the elderly couple took a stroll around their newly enhanced yard to see the end results, it was impossible for them not to acknowledge Derek.

Gia was relieved when they spoke to him with guarded courtesy. But it was noticeable how all of their gratitude and praise went to her alone.

Even then, Derek handled the situation with aplomb. He agreed with them that Gia had done a remarkable job and didn't seem in the least offended by their lack of gratitude for the backbreaking work he'd done all day.

When the older couple went inside, Gia said, "Thanks for everything you did today."

"You're welcome." He grinned as if her gratitude was payment enough.

"I'm surprised that you knew your way around this stuff."

"My grandmother raised my brothers, sisters, cousins and me—there are ten of us—and she was originally a farm girl, so she believed in chores for everybody. As a kid, I did yard work—among other things. All the boys in the family did—sexist, I know, but the girls had to do more dusting so I guess it evened out."

"The Bronsons told me that H. J. Camden's son, grandsons and granddaughters-in-law were killed in a plane crash—you were one of the ten great-grandchildren left...."

"I was. Left to GiGi—that's what we call our grandmother—and H.J. and Margaret and Louie Haliburton, who work for GiGi but who are really more like family than anything."

It wasn't how Gia—or the Bronsons—had pictured things. They had imagined the Camdens as growing up like royalty, not as having to do their chores like any other family.

"But even with ten kids around, the Camdens didn't have a troop of gardeners?" she asked.

He laughed. "Sure. A troop of seven able-bodied grandsons. We still trade off going over to help with the yard work even now—you're just lucky that this wasn't my week or I'd have been late getting here this morning."

"Well, I'm glad you weren't since no one else knew how to fix the lawnmower."

"That church minister was making the attempt, though," he reminded her. Then, after a pause, he said, "He wanted to take you to dinner tonight...."

The pastor had given it a second try.

"I didn't know anyone had overheard that," Gia said.

"Is he trying to convert you, or is he interested in more than that?" Derek asked with a hint of teasing to his tone.

Gia laughed. "I've wondered the same thing. I'm not exactly sure either way. But since he knows his congregation doesn't approve of him being with someone who's been divorced, it could be conversion."

"So you said no."

"Because I'm not interested in dating anyone for any reason."

Derek Camden nodded. "Then what would you say to going our separate ways to clean up then meeting for a nondate bite to eat—just because you and I seem to be the only two without plans tonight?" He leaned in so he could add confidentially, "You can tell me how you think I did with the Bronsons today and maybe give me some tips for improvement."

No.

It was a simple answer and the only one she knew she should give him.

But the wheels of Gia's mind instantly began to spin.

It was Saturday night.

She'd put in a long day.

Everyone else *had* gone off on dates like Tyson had, or dinners out with spouses.

Larry and Marion were inside fixing their own dinner, after which they would cozy up on their sofa with popcorn to watch an old movie—their Saturday-night-at-the-movies tradition upheld even though they could no longer afford to go to a theater.

And she was slated for a shower and sitting alone in front of the television, eating whatever leftovers were in her fridge.

Or she could shower and meet Derek Camden for a *bite to eat.* A nondate. Unlike what the minister had invited her to.

She hadn't been at all tempted to accept the minister's offer.

But Derek Camden's?

She just couldn't seem to bring herself to say no....

"Not a date," she clarified firmly, knowing even as she did that she was walking a fine line but really hating the thought of those leftovers in front of the TV....

"Not a date," he confirmed. "We can both wear whatever—shorts, T-shirts, anything comfortable. I won't pick you up. I won't open your car door. We'll just meet at the restaurant. I'll buy you dinner in exchange for tips on how better to win over these guys so they let me really help them," he said with a nod at the Bronsons' house. "And then we'll go our separate ways afterward."

She *did* want to encourage a truce between the Bronsons and this man in order to get the Bronsons as much aid from the Camdens as she could.

That was what put it over the top for her. She was doing this for the Bronsons....

"Okay," she agreed.

"What do you feel like eating—Italian, Mediterranean, Moroccan, Mexican, Chinese, sushi...?"

She closed her eyes to think about it and when she opened them he was grinning at her.

"Did that help you decide?" he asked with a laugh.

"I was just giving my stomach the chance to tell me what it wanted," she said as if it should have been obvious.

"And what did it tell you?" Another question within another laugh.

"Lemon chicken at the Red Lantern on Broadway."

"Your stomach is very specific," he teased. "No dessert?"

"Always dessert—that was actually the deciding vote. The Red Lantern has this really, really dark chocolate pudding—the lemon chicken is just what I have to eat to get to that."

He laughed again but there was something about it—appreciation or delight or something—that didn't make her feel as if he was making fun of her at all. "Of course—really, really dark chocolate pudding. Can you be there in an hour?"

"An hour," she confirmed, knowing that didn't leave her a lot of time.

But that lack of time ensured that she couldn't make this a bigger deal than it needed to be, so that was all she gave herself.

* * *

Gia didn't wear shorts—she wore khaki capris. But she did put on a simple red square-neck T-shirt with a red-and-white-striped tank top peeking from underneath it. Without much time to get ready, she'd washed her hair in a hurry, scrunched it and left it loose in order to spend some of that time applying blush, mascara, eyeliner and a glossy lipstick.

When she got to the Red Lantern she noted that Derek—who was waiting for her by leaning against his black sports car in the parking lot—had also not opted for shorts. Instead he was wearing jeans that were much better than what he'd worn to work in earlier today. But he, too, had gone with a T-shirt—a white V-neck with long sleeves that he'd pushed to his elbows.

He was freshly shaven, his hair was clean and casually perfect, and it didn't matter whether or not he'd put much thought into his attire; he still looked great.

She warned herself not to pay too much attention to that as she parked.

Having spotted her when she'd turned in from the street, he pushed off of his car and followed her all the way back to the only open space at the far end of the lot. As promised, he didn't open her car door for her, but he was waiting right there when she got out of her small hybrid sedan.

She caught him giving her the once-over, which prompted a small smile, as if he liked what he saw. But all he said was that he'd already gone in and put their names on the waiting list, so they should have a table shortly.

Gia wondered if he'd tipped the hostess in advance, because the place was crowded but all it took was him stepping up to the hostess station and giving his name for them to be led right to a table.

They ordered soon after sitting down, and once they'd been served their iced teas, he said, "So, how do you think I did today?"

"You were a lot of help," she assured him.

He laughed. "I don't mean how did I do with the work. I meant how did I do with the Bronsons."

"Oh. Well, no rocks were thrown and the hose wasn't turned on you, so I think that counts as a success at this point."

"You say that as if you half expected it to happen," he said with a laugh.

Gia shrugged. "You were the one who thought rocks might be thrown, so I didn't think that would happen. But the hose part was mentioned…."

His laugh had just a touch of alarm to it. "They talked about turning the hose on me?"

Gia shrugged again. "You know, what your family did to the Bronsons was pretty bad…. Awful, in fact…."

He sobered somewhat and admitted, "Actually, I might not know exactly what went on. It was 1968— my father and my uncle were only teenagers then, so it was my great-grandfather and my grandfather at the helm. But even when my father and my uncle grew up and were on board they all kept things completely separate—business was business, home was home. They *never* brought business home with them—"

"But still the Camdens have a reputation…."

"I know. Over the years we've heard the bad stuff that's been said about us. But H.J. always said it was nothing, not to take it seriously, that he'd never done anything wrong. And to us—" Derek took a turn at shrugging "—H.J. was our great-grandfather. He took care of us. He doted on us. That was all we knew from him. When anyone brought up something that was being said, he'd say that in business, in politics, in sports and in life there were wins and there were losses. And that whoever lost was never happy about it—that that was where the bad-mouthing came from and not to pay any attention to it."

"So you didn't," Gia said as their meal arrived and they began to eat.

"Not really. GiGi's take on it was that success came with a cost, and she guessed that having some negative things—she actually called them lies—said about us was that cost."

"But they aren't lies. I mean, I don't know about anything else, but they aren't lies when it comes to Larry and Marion."

"With the Bronsons, I don't know all the details, to be perfectly honest. I know that they owned a hotel—"

"The Larkspur," Gia supplied.

"It was built in the late 1800s."

"By Larry's great-great-grandfather," she filled in as they ate.

"And it was in the very heart of downtown Denver on a prime piece of real estate."

Again Gia offered information. "A prime piece of real estate that H. J. Camden wanted to build a store on."

"Right," Derek concurred. "But while the real-estate was prime, what was on it had gone downhill...." he said diplomatically.

"The Larkspur needed work," Gia conceded. "Larry and Marion admit that they hadn't had the time or money it needed because of Roddy—"

"Roddy? Who's Roddy?"

"Their son. You didn't know they had a son?"

"I didn't," Derek said.

"So you *don't* know everything," Gia muttered more to herself than to him.

"I don't," he answered. "In fact, I think it's probably safe to say that what I do know is only the tip of the iceberg, and even that I haven't known for long."

Gia wasn't quite sure what that meant but she didn't see a point in trying to figure it out.

Instead she said, "Roddy was born with a lot of congenital problems. Larry says the doctors were actually surprised that he lived, but he thinks that Marion willed him to. He was ill and severely mentally and physically handicapped. He died thirty years ago, long before I knew Larry and Marion—"

"How long have you known them?"

"Three years. As long as I've been in my house— that's when we met, when I moved in. But we got close fast. They were good to me at a time when I needed some—I don't know, some kindness, people who cared about me, some bolstering—and they did all that and... Well, they treated me like *I* was their kid."

But she didn't want to say more about herself so she went on telling him about the Bronsons. "They've talked a lot about Roddy, though, and I've seen a few photographs. He spent his life in a wheelchair—spinal issues made him sort of twisted and he couldn't walk. He couldn't talk or do anything for himself.... But he was their son and they loved him and they were committed to taking care of him themselves, which took a lot."

"I can imagine," Derek said sympathetically. "And that's where their time and money went."

"It was a struggle for them. Roddy's medical expenses were considerable and one of them needed to be with him all the time. And running a hotel is a round-the-clock operation, too, so they were stretched thin—although they never talk about it with any kind of complaint, it just was what it was."

"And what it was was difficult."

"I can't imagine it myself," Gia said. "But *inn keeping*—as they call it sometimes—was all they knew. The Larkspur was all they had. And they also had Roddy. So they did the best they could."

"And the hotel went downhill." His tone suggested that what he was learning didn't sit well with him.

"It had been in Larry's family since it was built. The Larkspur rivaled the Brown Palace and the Oxford, they tell me. And every generation that had managed it had made sure that it was updated and expanded to keep up with the times. Including Larry and Marion—"

"Until they had Roddy."

"For a while they had some family—parents—who helped. But when they lost them, they were on their own with Roddy and with the Larkspur and they just couldn't maintain the standard. So yes, it went downhill. And that was when H. J. Camden swooped in."

"He offered to buy them out."

"In order to tear the Larkspur down and build a Camden store. Of course the Bronsons said no."

"And he increased the offer," Derek said, stating a fact, not being confrontational at all, merely supplying what he *did* know about things.

"It still wasn't a great offer, but it wouldn't have mattered. The Larkspur meant something to the Bronsons. More than the fact that it was their only asset and their only way to make a living. They were going through the process of having it qualified as an historic landmark, which would not only have protected it but would have brought in restoration funds. And they're sure it would have happened if not for H. J. Camden."

The waiter came to remove their plates, and Derek ordered Gia's chocolate pudding and sorbet for himself for dessert.

When the waiter left, Derek didn't comment on her last statement and she had the sense that he didn't know what to say to it. But Gia felt as if she was finally letting the Bronsons be heard, so she continued.

"H. J. Camden had political clout and the money to buy influence. Getting the Larkspur declared an historic landmark was going well until he decided he wanted the property it was on. Then all of a sudden the whole qualification process stalled. And at the same time, state inspectors became overly interested in the Larkspur and cited it with enough health and building code violations to have it condemned—"

"Literally condemned?"

"Literally. Inspectors said it was going to fall down around them and not only couldn't they stay open for business, they couldn't live there themselves anymore, either. And that was absolutely not true—they had an independent contractor look at it and he confirmed that it wasn't in that kind of shape—"

"And the independent contractor's report didn't carry any weight?"

"Not when he was suddenly hired by Hank Camden to build Camden stores out of state and the report disappeared."

Derek flinched slightly at that.

"All the hotel really needed was what the Bronsons' house needs now—paint, plumbing and electrical repairs and updating, maybe a new kitchen—but it wasn't falling down around their ears."

Derek's frown caused his brows to twitch together, suggesting he was troubled by what Gia had told him. But he gave no response.

She went on without one. "Larry challenged the rulings, but without the independent contractor's report, without the money to hire another one or to hire a good lawyer, he was no match for what he found himself up against. He lost the challenges, the Bronsons couldn't afford repairs to address the inflated building code violations and they had no choice but to close their doors and take the Camden offer. An offer that was mere pennies on the dollar of the initial offer."

Derek was scowling by the time the waiter served their desserts. But still Gia didn't let up.

"The Bronsons were left with no property, very little money and mounting expenses for Roddy. Not being able to live at the hotel meant they were even homeless. So they used the lion's share of the money from the buyout to get the house they're in now—"

"Over forty years ago—shouldn't that have been paid off years back?" he asked between bites.

"Spoken like a finance guy. Actually, they used the money from the hotel to buy the house outright—it made them feel a little more secure after the rug being pulled out from under them. But without the hotel, they had to go to work for other people, and Roddy went through health crisis after health crisis that would keep them both away from their jobs, so they'd eventually be let go. Over the years the house had to be mortgaged and refinanced and refinanced and second mortgaged—"

"So it isn't paid off."

Again Gia was hesitant to reveal too much of the Bronson's vulnerability, just in case, so she merely shrugged once more in answer and concluded what she was saying.

"No matter how you look at it—and certainly it's the way they look at it—because of what H. J. Camden did to get what he wanted, rather than being the owners of their family legacy and a Denver landmark, the Bronsons saw that legacy and landmark get bulldozed. They ended up having a life of hardship and money problems, and age and no extra retirement funds and trying to make it on a fixed income have only compounded those problems."

Gia watched as Derek rubbed his sculpted jawline in a gesture that conveyed discomfort. "Wow. Most of that is news to me," he said somberly.

Most of it, but not all of it....

Gia noted that he didn't say which parts were *not* news to him.

Never admit to anything—that was legal advice she'd overheard given to the Grants.

That and to put some money into a worthy cause to make themselves look better whenever ugly rumors or accusations surfaced....

"So what you're saying is that the Bronsons took the higher ground today by *not* throwing rocks or turning the hose on me," Derek said then, clearly making a joke to ease some of the tension.

"Kind of," Gia answered.

He nodded as if he understood and didn't necessarily disagree.

"I'm sorry if I got a little carried away," she apologized, taking a deep breath and consciously toning it down because she realized that her own outrage on the Bronsons' behalf might have made her sound heated.

"It's okay. I wanted to hear it from the Bronsons' perspective."

"Oh, they get a whole lot more irate when they tell it...."

He laughed somewhat helplessly. "Better it came from you, then," he joked.

The waiter brought their check at that moment and when he'd left, Derek said, "Well, today we made a little headway—we did the Bronsons' yard. Next Saturday we'll work on the inside of the house. And after that we'll do whatever else needs to be done."

Whatever else needs to be done was not a specific commitment to anything. And yet Gia had the sense that today wasn't the beginning and end of his involvement, that he honestly did intend to follow this through.

But we'll see, she told herself, unwilling and unable to trust him too much.

He paid the bill, refusing to allow Gia to leave even the tip, and they left the restaurant.

Darkness had fallen, and in the parking lot he bypassed his own car to walk her all the way to hers—a date-like courtesy that Gia appreciated only for the safety factor.

Or so she told herself.

"Can I ask a favor?" Derek said as they reached her car and she unlocked the door.

"You can ask...."

"I'm truly sorry for what happened to the Bronsons no matter what caused the life they've had and the position they're in now. And I'll take whatever hit they want to throw—rocks, the hose turned on me... I know that one way or another, the reality for them is that I'm a Camden and a Camden store sits in place of the hotel that—had things gone differently—they could still be benefitting from. The hotel that was their family legacy...."

He paused before he added, "But would *you* try to

keep in mind that I wasn't even a twinkle in anybody's eye at the time this went down? That I didn't have a single thing to do with it, and that now I'm just trying to help these people the same way you are?"

Gia didn't immediately respond.

The parking lot was dimly lit, but they were standing near enough for her to still see his face—which seemed to get better looking the more she saw of it—and to still look into his striking blue eyes. And she openly studied it all, thinking about her ex, about his family, about how good they'd been at making themselves appear innocent when they were anything but.

And yet...

Derek was right. He hadn't had a part in any of what had happened to the Bronsons. He couldn't have had.

Which didn't mean he wasn't responsible for similar things that could be going on now. But it did mean that she couldn't blame him for what went on in the past.

So she conceded to that much. "I'll try to keep in mind that you didn't have anything to do with the lousy deal the Bronsons got."

But she wouldn't completely trust him, either.

She couldn't. Not for the Bronsons' sake, and not for her own.

"Thank you," he said. "Because not only didn't I have anything to do with it, I feel as badly for those people as you do."

Maybe she just wanted to believe that, but it somehow had the ring of truth to it. And the fact that he felt bad for the Bronsons, that he had what appeared to be genuine compassion and empathy for them, was more than she could say she'd ever seen from her ex or his family. So it bought him a slight concession from her.

But only a slight one.

Because feeling bad that his family did something wrong but still managed to get what it was after was not quite the same as that wrong never being done in the first place. At least as far as she was concerned.

It also wasn't the same as openly admitting that a wrong had been committed, renouncing whoever had committed it or relinquishing all the gains that had been made because of it.

"The best we can do now is try to get them out of the position they're in," she concluded.

He nodded and smiled an engaging smile before he said, "And they think the sun rises and sets with you. Every time I was within earshot today, they were talking about how wonderful you are. You're like the daughter they never had. You're a gift from God. They don't know what they'd do without you...." He shook his head as if in amazement at the pure number of accolades he'd overheard. "They *love* you."

"I think of them as a gift to me, too," she said. "It's one of those when-a-door-closes-a-window-opens things."

Derek nodded again, accepting that without questioning exactly what she meant.

Instead, he seemed more intent on studying her the way she'd studied him moments earlier. He seemed to appreciate the sight as much as she had, because another small smile appeared on his handsome face.

A small smile that drew her attention to his mouth. To such supple-looking lips...

And somehow she just knew he would be a good kisser. Though she had no idea why the thought crossed her mind.

Or why she was suddenly wishing—just a little—that he wouldn't be quite as chivalrous as he was being and actually kiss her good-night to let her test her theory....

But he didn't.

And he was true to his word—he also didn't make any move to open her door for her, so Gia finally did it herself, knowing she needed to go home and escape any kind of kissing thoughts whatsoever.

"So next Saturday," she said as she got in, attempting to neutralize the effect he was having on her.

He stepped up to close her door. "I'll be there," he assured her as she rolled down her window. "Text me a time."

"I'll send out a blanket reminder," she said as she started her engine.

"And I'll see you then. Have a nice week..." he said, stepping away from the car after a slap to the roof.

"You, too. And thanks for dinner...and your help today."

He merely raised his chin to that and stayed where he was, watching as she backed out of the parking spot, waving as she drove off.

It was a wave that Gia returned only half-heartedly, but not because of anything to do with him.

She was just aggravated with herself.

For feeling suddenly like a week was a very, very long while to wait to see him again....

Chapter Four

"Hey, Tommy, how's the foot? Jeanine—I like the haircut! Mitch, I owe you a ten spot—you were right about Dallas on Sunday. Tammy, how are you doin' today? I was told our fearless leader was in here somewhere...."

Gia was at the back of one of the Health Now greenhouses on Friday when she heard the greetings to her coworkers. It didn't take her more than a split second to recognize Derek Camden's voice carrying through the greenery, and another split second to recall that he'd met those particular coworkers doing the Bronsons' yard work.

What she hadn't been aware of was how familiar he'd become with them all. And she couldn't help being impressed by what he noticed and remembered, and how friendly he sounded. He'd also impressed her coworkers, if their warm responses to him were any indication because they all greeted him in return as if he was their favorite person, the last of them informing him of her location and that she was planting gingko.

"Hey there!" he said when he finally found her.

"Hey there yourself," Gia answered without masking her surprise to see him, wiping her hands on a damp cloth as she turned from her pots, seeds and soil.

She'd spent the entire week fighting constant thoughts of him, and she could have kicked herself when the very first thing that had popped into her mind when she'd woken up this morning was that there was only another twenty-four hours until she was going to see him again. But having him show up at work was just a shock.

And then an unwarranted disappointment when it occurred to her that he was probably there to make an excuse for why he *wouldn't* be at the Bronsons' tomorrow....

"What are you doing here? Oh, wait, careful! Don't lean against that, you'll get dirt on your suit," she warned before he had the chance to answer.

He glanced down at his suit coat, which was tan but had a mauve cast to it, and brushed away the dirt he'd rubbed against before she'd stopped him.

And in that moment, Gia took in the full image of the tall, broad-shouldered man dressed for *his* work in a suit that couldn't have been better tailored, a dress shirt that was off-white with that same mysterious mauve cast and a brown and mauve tie knotted at his throat.

She registered that he looked jaw-droppingly terrific, and then pushed that thought out of her head.

Which might not have been the best thing, because what replaced it was the sudden awareness of her own appearance.

Today was planting day—a day spent in the heat of the greenhouse. And since it required nothing other than working with soil, seeds and plants, she was dressed in worn-out sandals, jean shorts and a tank top, and her hair was a curly geyser bursting from a rubber band at the top of her head to keep it off her neck. Plus, there wasn't any use applying makeup that would melt in the greenhouse heat, so she hadn't.

It was not how she wanted to be seen by him, and a wave of self-consciousness struck her.

"I came to see if I could take you to lunch."

"I can't go anywhere with you dressed like that and me like this!" she blurted out.

He looked her up and down and grinned. "I don't know about me, but you're kind of adorable. You just look summery—what's wrong with that? We'll go someplace casual, with a patio where we can eat al fresco."

From behind the Echinacea, Jeanine said, "Go, Gia."

She *had* brought a shirt to put on over the tank top to go home....

But that wasn't going to upgrade her look much.

"Come on," Derek urged. "Get me out of this heat—I wanted to talk to you about the Bronsons."

So he hadn't come for her.

Gia knew it was stupid, but that disappointed her, too.

"If you can't make it tomorrow just say it—"

"That's not what I want to talk about—I'll be there tomorrow. But that's part of what I need to go over with you."

"It's time for lunch anyway, you might as well," Jeanine contributed.

Gia knew that Derek had to be more and more uncomfortable in the greenhouse heat, and since he just wanted to talk about the Bronsons, why should she care what she was wearing? So she gave in. "Okay, but nothing fancy—there's a sandwich place down the street with a few tables outside. Maybe we could just do that."

"Nothing fancy, sandwiches are fine," he agreed.

"I have a shirt I can put on. Let's go out back here," she said, leading him to a rear door and ushering him to the outdoor gardens.

"There's more out here?"

"And more greenhouses, too," Gia told him, pointing to the other two built around the perimeters of the outdoor garden.

"Greenhouses to grow in year-round, this garden to grow in the summer months, huh?"

"Right. We're watching for predictions of the first frost—we'll harvest just before that happens and then close these gardens down for winter. But right now—" She bent down and said to the pale purple flowers, "You're beautiful, aren't you?"

"You talk to your plants...."

"They're living things," she said.

"That smell like—"

"It's thyme. We use it in antiseptic and antifungal creams, and in cough medicine. It's good for bronchial infections. The leaves can be made into a tea, too."

"Also good in food," he supplied.

"Also good in food," she confirmed.

"So you grow all this?" he asked as Gia led him along the path through the plants and into the main building.

"We do. They're our babies, we plant them and nurse them along, then harvest and turn them over to production where some of them are ground and put into capsules or tablets, or pressed for their oils, or whatever can be done with them."

"And this stuff works like medicine?" he asked skeptically.

"This *stuff* has been around longer than contemporary medicine. It's what people used before there were chemicals. Sometimes the effects are more subtle or they take a little while to build up before they work, but rather than take chemicals to get rid of heartburn, give me gum or a peppermint leaf to chew, or an orange to eat, or a pill that doesn't have anything in it but orange oil."

"And those things work?"

"You'll never know until you try them," she challenged as they went into her small office. "Sometimes a spoonful of vinegar works, too."

"So you're anti–contemporary medicine?" he asked.

"No. But I'll always try something natural before I'll go the other route," she said as she took the tailored white blouse draped on her desk chair and put it on, buttoning it over her tank top. "And there are a lot of things that work as preventatives, too. Like the gingko in the greenhouse—that's good for the brain and the memory," she said, pointing to her head. "I take it every day."

He grinned again. "Is that what makes your hair so curly."

"No, that's genetic," she said with a bit of a grimace.

"What? You don't like it?"

"It kind of has a life of its own." She wished she'd worn it some way that tamed it a little more today, but there was nothing she could do about it now.

His grin just got bigger and he reached to gently bounce his palm off the top of the geyser. "A wild life of its own—I think it's great."

Not sure she believed that, Gia just made a face and took her purse from her desk drawer before pointing at the door.

Blouse or no blouse, she still felt woefully underdressed at his side as she guided him to the sandwich shop she'd mentioned.

It was a place everyone from Health Now frequented, so the owner knew her by sight. After placing their orders, Gia slid the donation jar next to the cash register toward herself and said, "I might as well take this with me today, Nick. It's the last jar I have out and I'm going to the bank later. Since we've started to use the money, I'll deposit it. Thanks for letting me leave it here, though."

"For you, anytime. My kids had better take so much care of me when I'm that age. Or maybe I'll have to come get you."

"I'm always right up the block," Gia assured him as they accepted their drinks and meatball sandwiches.

Derek carried the tray with everything on it so Gia could take the gallon-size pickle jar that was three quarters full—mostly with change, but with a few dollar bills in sight, too.

They took everything out to one of the four small tables on the sidewalk in front of the shop. As they sat down, Derek said, "First the dessert shop, now the sandwich shop—do you just make friends wherever you go?"

Gia shrugged. "I'm a creature of habit. I see the same people over and over again. We talk. I get to know them and they get to know me."

"And like you."

She shrugged again. "Maybe. But it takes me going in over and over again. One day with you and everybody I work with seems to think you're great."

He laughed. "Why do you say that as if I did something wrong?"

"Oh, no, I didn't mean that." She'd just been thinking about her ex-husband's surface charm and what it had concealed and wondering if the same was true of

Derek. "I'm only saying that with me it takes some time and repeat business before I get where you got with the people I work with in a single day."

"With everyone but the Bronsons."

Who had cause to be wary because they'd seen beneath the surface of the Camdens.

"What about tomorrow did you want to talk to me about—if you're still coming?" Gia asked, changing the subject as they began eating.

"I wanted to let you know that I've hired a crew of professional plumbers and electricians to check everything out and fix whatever they might find wrong."

"We can't pay for that."

"I'm paying for it. After seeing the age of that house and the shape it's in, I thought it should be inspected—especially the wiring, since it could be a fire hazard. And I know you're trying to get everything done in a hurry, so there will be big enough crews coming in to do just about anything that needs to be done in the one day."

That had to cost a fortune, and while she wanted to believe it was purely an act of generosity, she couldn't help recalling the Bronsons' concerns about his interest in the place and getting slightly suspicious.

"You don't want their house, right?" she asked as he took his first bite of sandwich.

He chuckled and frowned at the same time. "Why would I want their house?" he asked when he'd finished chewing.

"Your family took their hotel. Larry and Marion are a little worried that now—"

"We want their house?" he said in disbelief. "Do they just think we want to persecute them for some reason? That we're targeting them?"

"You aren't, are you?"

"No, of course not. There isn't a reason in the world we would. In fact, after hearing that their house is mortgaged, the other thing I wanted out of this lunch today was to get a better idea of what their financial situation really is. Are they deeply in debt? Are they behind in their mortgage payments? How much is the mortgage as a whole…?"

Gia purposely took a bite of her sandwich so that her mouth was full and she couldn't answer. She wanted to buy herself time to gauge what to do.

She hadn't been forthcoming with him on this subject before out of paranoia that the Bronsons might somehow be right in worrying that there was a self-serving motivation behind the Camdens' help.

But it just didn't seem reasonable that they would want the Bronsons' house for any reason. And since the Bronsons needed a lot more help than the jars of spare change like the one at her feet could provide, she decided to trust him. A little anyway. And just with some information.

So when her mouth was empty she said, "The only debt they have is on their house. But they just can't keep up the payments anymore. They're in arrears and the bank has notified them that if they don't come up with the back payments, foreclosure proceedings are going to start."

"So you decided to mow the lawn and paint the walls?" he said as if he didn't understand her thinking.

"I decided to try to raise money for them. My fantasy was to raise enough to pay the back payments, then maybe get the house refinanced so the payments could be more what they could afford—"

"So shouldn't every penny be going toward the back payments?"

"I waited to see how close I was coming. But unfortunately it wasn't close enough. With what I've raised so far all I can do is make a dent in the back payments—unless the yard sale brings in a *lot,* and I know that isn't likely. So I'm going with the contingency plan—"

"Which is to paint the walls and mow the lawn?" he said, still confused.

"If I can't pay the back payments completely, then the next best thing is to pay enough to stall the foreclosure so the house can be sold—"

"Ah, I see—so you're putting some of the money you've raised into getting the place in better shape in order to sell it."

"Right. And the better shape it's in, the better the chance of getting a higher price, which—I'm hoping—means that the Bronsons would come out with a small amount of cash."

"Then what? If they can't stay in their house, what happens to them?"

She told him about her plan to move them into her basement apartment.

"Really? You'd do that?"

"A couple they knew was in the same situation a few years ago. Social Services ended up involved because they were elderly and didn't have any family. But Social Services put the wife in one nursing home and the husband in a different one—both of them not very nice places—because it was just a matter of available beds. After being married for over fifty years, those people died without ever seeing each other again. And I won't let that happen to Larry and Marion."

"So you'll move them into your basement apartment and be responsible for them, and what? Charge them rent they can afford?"

"I couldn't take money from them. I'll just move them in—"

"And become responsible for them."

"I'll take care of them whether they're next door or in my basement. It's just that they don't *want* to lose their house. They want to stay in it, and I can understand that, so I'm giving it the best shot I can—and who knows, maybe the yard sale *will* put us over the top. But in the meantime I have to be realistic and get the place in selling condition, too. I'm not using much of the money—all the labor and most of the materials are donated—but it has to be done...."

He nodded and seemed to be lost in thought as he finished his sandwich.

Then he said, "Have you told me everything? Because it gets a little bleaker every time I persuade you to talk about it, and I really am trying to see the whole picture so I know what to do for them."

"That's the whole picture," Gia said as she wadded up the paper her own sandwich had been wrapped in, hoping she hadn't put the Bronsons farther out on a limb by revealing it all to him. "They live a simple—and *really* frugal—life. It's just gotten away from them."

"And they honestly don't have any other debt—credit cards, a car?"

Gia shook her head. "Their car is twenty years old and mostly sits in the garage—Larry drives a little if he has to and if it isn't too far, but that's it. They have a credit card for emergencies, but *only* for emergencies. I put them on my cell phone plan with a freebie phone so they could cancel their landline and cut that expense. For Larry's birthday I paid off his dental bill because the payments they were making to the dentist were strapping them, so that's gone. It's just the house, utilities, food and medical stuff—they live hand-to-mouth…"

"And apparently have friends who do, too…" he said, frowning again.

"People who live on a fixed income have trouble making ends meet—it's a fact of life."

"An ugly one."

Gia didn't say anything to that, wondering if it was ugly enough to send him running.

But then his eyes in all their blue glory looked squarely into hers and he vowed, "We're going to take care of this."

Then her ex and his family flashed through her mind and something else occurred to her.

"There's not going to be anything in it for you, right?" she said firmly. "Because the Bronsons would be furious if you used them to make the Camdens look like saints for lending a hand. If that's what's behind this I'll throw rocks at you myself."

He held up both hands, palms outward. "Nothing in it for us, I promise. How would it make us look good to say we're helping out a couple who might not be in the position they're in had a Camden store not gone where their hotel used to be?"

"And I'd stir up that whole story, too," she warned.

"There's not going to be a reason to," he assured her. "This is your deal—we're just trying to give some of the help you've asked for."

Gia decided to take a chance and trust him. While her past experience gave her reason to be wary, so far there was no indication that he had ulterior motives where the Bronsons were concerned.

"Okay," she conceded. Then, because it was true, she said, "I should get back to work."

"What, no chocolate dessert at lunch?" he teased, showing that he hadn't taken offense at her suspicion.

She appreciated that and leaned forward to say under her breath, "Nick only has some Italian cookies that aren't very good."

"I saw them in the case—they're also not chocolate," Derek whispered back. "Could that be the reason you think they're not very good?"

"It's possible," she conceded.

"How about somewhere else? We could go back the way we came and around the corner to the bakery.... Lava cake..."

He thought he was tempting her with chocolate. And while that was always a temptation for her, she discovered that it was equally as tempting to prolong this time with him despite the apprehensions he aroused in her just by being who he was and coming from the family he came from.

There was just some kind of chemistry that got activated in her with this guy that she wished she could deactivate. At least she could try not to indulge it, so she held the line.

"I really can't," she insisted.

"Well, I guess I'll get to see you tomorrow, so I'll let you go today," he said, making her wonder if he was merely being charming or if he actually wanted to spend more time with her.

It doesn't matter! she silently shouted at herself.

Derek took their tray and dumped the lunch remnants in the nearby trash, and then turned to pick up the jar of money.

"This can't be lightweight. Let me carry it." Gia didn't argue because it *was* heavy, and she hadn't been looking forward to toting it herself. But Derek carried it under one arm, against his hip, and didn't seem to exert himself too much.

"So do you grow everything your company needs in the gardens here? Right in the middle of the city?" he asked as they headed back to Health Now, clearly making an effort to put things securely back on more neutral ground.

"No," Gia answered. "This is just where the company started. We expanded about four years ago to an area outside of Broomfield. We produce about a quarter of what's needed here and the rest there."

"Does that mean that you work in Broomfield, too?"

"It does. All the offices are in Denver—Broomfield is just greenhouses and another outdoor garden that's about the size of a football field—but the botanists and horticulturists go back and forth to care for the plants. That's where Peggy and Marshall are today—you met them last Saturday, too."

"Right, I remember—Peggy is the really, really skinny woman and Marshall is—"

"The really, really *not* skinny guy," Gia supplied for him.

"He's a big man," Derek agreed with a laugh. "Knows a lot about music and computers."

"Yes, he does—his two passions outside of work." Again Gia was surprised that Derek had bothered to get so friendly with everyone.

Maybe that was what she was responding to, she told herself. Maybe it was just his general friendliness—the same general friendliness he showed to everyone—and she'd been out of the single world for so long that she somehow read more into it than was there.

The possibility made her feel all the more ridiculous for having thought about him as much as she had for the past week. For having made-up, flirty conversations with him in her head. Flirty conversations that were so much wittier than anything she'd pulled off today....

He insisted on taking the jar all the way inside to her office, where she assured him it was safe to leave it on her desk.

But once he'd done that and she was waiting for him to leave so she could take her blouse off again, he instead turned his focus onto her.

"Thanks for going to lunch with me today," he said.

"Even if I gave you a hard time?"

He grinned. "There does always seem to be a minute or two when we're together when you narrow those big brown eyes and look at me like I'm the enemy. You're just not sure about me yet, are you?" he asked.

Gia shrugged.

And that made him grin. "You're not," he said, as if it amused him. But also with what sounded like affection.

Or maybe she was just imagining it.

She was probably just imagining it.

Along with the sense she kept having that there were small sparks shooting between them as he studied her face.

"You were on my mind a lot this past week," he said then. His mouth eased into a small, thoughtful smile as his gaze rose somewhat and he added, "Must be the hair." His blue eyes returned to hers. "But it made me want to touch base with you on our own just a little before we're in the middle of everything and everybody tomorrow...."

So that was what had prompted the lunch....

Gia nodded because she suddenly couldn't think straight enough to say anything. Instead, her thoughts were drifting to the idea of him kissing her....

Kissing her...

That was something else she'd thought way, way too much about since last Saturday night.

Something that certainly had no place here and now, at work....

And yet he was looking at her so intently that it caused her to actually entertain the notion that he might be thinking about it, too.

That couldn't be...

But he wasn't even making small talk anymore. He was standing there—dashingly handsome in a suit that probably cost as much as her car—just looking into her eyes.

Then down at her mouth....

The outer office had been empty when they'd come in. Everyone was probably in the lunchroom, and her office couldn't be seen from there. Plus, she'd probably be able to hear something if anyone came back....

Her chin went up a fraction of an inch as she looked into those astonishingly blue eyes...and was shocked to find herself ready.

Ready to be kissed by someone other than Elliot.

Ready to be kissed by this man she hadn't been able to get out of her head for two solid weeks now....

And she really, honestly thought he was going to do it as she watched him move forward.

This is crazy!

And yet she didn't back off....

But then Derek did. He caught himself and stood a little straighter.

Without the sound of anyone coming, Gia realized. Without any indication that she would have rejected him. Still, he'd backed off.

He made a sort of confused, mildly troubled face and

smiled a tight-lipped smile before saying, "So I guess I'll see you tomorrow."

"At the Bronsons', bright and early. One of their church friends is taking them out for the day so we can just work. All of us."

Somehow that *we* had had an intimate inflection so she'd felt the need to amend it.

He smiled more openly and she knew he was about to make a joke even before he said, "What was I in danger of this week—a ladder getting kicked out from under me? Being pushed down stairs?"

Gia got hold of herself and said, "No threats this round. You're safe."

He smiled as if he wasn't so sure about that.

Then he took a step toward her office door and said, "I'll let you get back to your plants and saving lives with leaves."

"Saving lives with leaves," she parroted. "Hmm… that could be one of our slogans."

"I don't need credit for that, either," he joked, making her smile.

And like him.

Even though she didn't want to.

"See you tomorrow," he said as he went out.

"See you tomorrow," she answered.

Then she was alone in her office, needing a few minutes to recover before she could go out and see anyone.

Wondering during that time exactly what had just happened between them.

And if not being kissed in a very long time might have robbed her of the ability to read the signs….

Chapter Five

"Oh, hi," Gia said, stopping cold in the doorway of the Bronsons' bedroom on Saturday morning.

When she'd assigned everyone to the work that needed to be done today, it had taken a strong force of will not to team herself up with Derek. Instead, she'd put him with Jeanine to paint the guest room across the hall. So she was surprised to see him in the room she was supposed to be painting with Tyson.

Jeanine was single and actively looking for a mate. Although it had secretly not sat well with Gia, she'd forced herself to put the two together. She'd reasoned that if something got started between them then maybe she could stomp out whatever it was that was going on with her in regards to Derek.

But there he was, managing to look good even in a pair of ragged old jeans and a plain white undershirt-sort-of-T-shirt, taking tarps out of their packaging.

"Hi," he answered her greeting.

"You know the guest room is across the hall..." she informed him.

"Yeah, I did some rearranging—did *you* know that Tyson is dating the blonde bombshell from your marketing department?"

"I introduced them, so yes, I knew that. Minna..."

Minna, who was wearing short shorts and a bandeau top that barely contained her ample chest, while Gia was in throwaway jeans torn at the knee and an equally ratty T-shirt so it wouldn't matter if she got paint splattered.

Minna, whose long blond hair was flowing free, while Gia's had to be pulled back into a twist that hardly contained her geyser of curls.

Minna, who, yes, looked like a blonde bombshell while Gia felt as if she faded into the woodwork in comparison, despite the fact that she'd done her makeup today.

"Plus," she added, "Tyson is not only my best friend, he temporarily lives in the apartment on the upper floor of my house, so there isn't much I *don't* know about him."

"Well, it seemed like they'd want to work together. And last week Jeanine and that Adam Smythe from the Botanical Gardens were getting pretty friendly—I thought Jeanine would rather paint with him than with me. So we made some changes. Is that okay, or did you have your heart set on working with Tyson? He said he didn't think it mattered who worked where as long as everything got done."

Tyson had spent most of the past week with Minna and Gia had hardly seen him. She'd thought a day of painting together would give them a chance to catch up. But more important, she'd counted on him to provide her with a safety net from Derek. She hadn't been able to talk to Tyson, though, and let him know that it felt risky for her to be in close quarters with Derek all day, so he couldn't have known that was her plan.

But she certainly couldn't tell Derek that. Or make a fuss over harmless changes in the roster.

"It doesn't matter," she said, hoping she sounded as indifferent as she was trying to sound.

And at the same time, she wondered if Derek had purposely switched the teams to be with her.

That was unlikely, she told herself.

But it still didn't calm the tiny wave of excitement that it was even remotely possible.

"What's with the bed? It has some…topography…" he said then, pointing his chin at it as he stood at the foot taking the tarps out of their packages and setting them on the floor.

"Oh, I rigged it," Gia said, finally going all the way into the room. "Larry has reflux problems when he lies down flat, so I got him a foam wedge to prop him up a little. Marion has a bad shoulder that doesn't bother her if her arm on that side has something to rest on, and an arthritic hip that hurts less if her knees are bent some when she sleeps. So I put a piece of foam under the mattress pad on the edge of the bed for her arm, and another piece where her knees go. I know it looks weird—they call it the Frankenstein bed—but it works."

He angled his head in the direction she'd just come from. "And the *rigging* on the light switch? I saw that when I moved the dresser away from the wall…."

"If the dresser goes against that wall, they have more space in here, but it covered the light switch. So I fixed it so the light switch is usable with the dresser in front of it."

"Your idea, too?"

"Yeah," she said, taking the wrapping off the roll of tape she was going to use to paint edges.

"Inventive."

"It's just a few pieces of foam and a stick with a hole in one end and knob on the other," Gia said. Then, when he shook out one of the tarps to put over the bed, she added, "Let's take the pictures off the walls and put them on the bed first, then cover it all."

"Good idea."

There was a gallery of framed photographs on one wall, but when Gia met Derek there he was looking at them rather than taking them down.

"These must be their parents," Derek observed of the black-and-white pictures that showed people with Roaring Twenties hairstyles and fashion.

Gia pointed out which was Larry's family and which was Marion's. "And that's Marion with her parents when she was five or six." Then she pointed to another cluster of snapshots. "That's Roddy."

"Oooh, he doesn't look well," Derek said sympathetically.

"Even as a newborn he wasn't just pink and perfect. But they loved him the way he was."

Gia took down the photos and laid them extra carefully on the bed.

"This must be Larry and Marion's wedding picture," Derek said as he brought another black-and-white photograph to set beside those of Roddy.

Gia glanced at it. "I can never get over how young Marion looks in that picture. When I say that to her, she jokes that she was Larry's child bride," Gia said affectionately. "But even Larry was only nineteen."

"How did they meet?" Derek asked as they removed

the remainder of the photos, placed them on the bed and then covered everything with a tarp.

"They met at the Trocadero Ballroom in the old Elitch Gardens," Gia said, referring to one of Denver's original entertainment centers that had included an amusement park and a renowned theater and ballroom.

"Some big band was there," Gia went on. "I've never heard of it, but they actually have an old album of the music—and a record player to play it—and sometimes they put it on and dance to it even now. Anyway, they were there separately with friends and none of them knew each other. But all of Larry's friends had asked Marion to dance and been turned down. Then Larry strolled right across the middle of the dance floor— that's how Marion puts it—and she says he was the one she was waiting for."

"She wasn't afraid that he'd get discouraged by all the other rejections and never ask?"

"Larry says she was giving him the eye from across the room, so he thought he'd have better luck. Marion denies it, but when she does Larry shakes his head to let you know she's lying and she just laughs."

"And they've been married how long?" Derek asked with some amusement in his voice.

"Since a week after Marion graduated from high school when she was seventeen—this year was their seventieth anniversary."

"Wow," Derek said as they draped tarps over the dresser and lined the floor with them.

"I know, hard to imagine, isn't it? And they're still so good together. Even after all they've gone through, one's eyes light up when the other comes into a room, they still flirt with each other and—"

"Sleep in the same lumpy bed."

Gia laughed and hoped she didn't sound like a sappy romantic when she echoed, "They still sleep in the same lumpy bed." Then she said, "And I catch them holding hands just sitting on the couch watching TV sometimes. Marion says Larry has never forgotten a birthday or an anniversary, and I don't know what she does on Valentine's Day, but whatever it is, he always says that she's never forgotten one of those either, and then he wiggles his eyebrows and makes Marion blush."

Derek laughed. "Seriously? Even now, in their eighties, after seventy years of marriage?"

"Seriously. I make sure to give this place a wide berth that whole day and night."

He laughed harder. "Seems like that might be wise."

"And they still kiss…." Gia marveled as they began to put tape around the bedroom window.

"Aren't they supposed to?"

"I don't know," she mused. "Sometimes people who haven't been married anywhere near as long have to force their spouse to kiss them hello or goodbye or… you know, anytime that it isn't going to lead to…sex…. And eventually they just give up trying…"

"Is that the voice of experience?" he asked gently.

It was. But she'd basically been thinking out loud of her own marriage in comparison to Larry and Marion's, and she wasn't willing to let Derek know that, so she merely said, "I just mean that it's still obvious that Larry and Marion really do love each other and enjoy each other's company. They aren't like a lot of people who've been together for a while—they aren't just roommates. They don't bicker. It isn't as if they're only together for convenience or out of habit but don't really like each other—"

"Yeah, I guess I know what you're talking about. I've

seen couples like that, too. The spark is gone, they're bored, there's no excitement or they actually seem to *dis*like each other, and you wonder why they're together at all."

"Larry and Marion still talk. They still laugh together. They still think of each other first. They aren't even impatient with the small things that can get annoying—Larry will say something silly and Marion thinks it's endearing, or Marion will repeat the same story over and over and every time she does Larry will just say that she tells it so well. They're just…happy to have each other, I guess. Even after all this time."

"I envy that," he admitted. "It's how I'd like to end up."

Gia laughed. "Is that what you were thinking when you went out with Tyson's nutty cousin Sharon? That you could find it with her?" she teased as he pried open the paint can and poured some into the tray.

Derek didn't seem to take offense because he laughed, too. "Hey, you never know…Sharon might not have been my Marion, but it beats some of the women I go out with who make me feel like I'm watching paint dry when they talk."

That would probably be me, Gia thought.

But what she said was, "So only psychics and mediums and vampire witches for you!"

He laughed again. "Vampire witches? I don't *think* I've ever dated one of those."

"But you'd probably like the fangs and magic spells, right?"

More laughing. "Now you're starting to sound like my grandmother."

That couldn't be good….

So Gia opted to change the subject and handed Derek

the roller and the extension pole that went with it. "How about you work on the ceiling while I start the walls?"

He agreed, and as they went to work he said, "So what was the big band that brought Larry and Marion together?"

After telling him the name, they began to talk about what kind of music they each liked. That led to a discussion of favorite television programs and movies, travel destinations, food—besides chocolate—colors, seasons, holidays and on and on.

To subjects Gia only hoped didn't make her sound like his grandmother....

The day flew by for Gia. When it was over, she left Tyson to oversee the finishing work and cleanup so she could run home to do some last-minute preparations for the barbecue she'd invited everyone to afterward.

Seizing the opportunity that afforded her, she quickly changed out of her paint-splattered clothes and into a pair of black capris with a tailored black-and-white flowered blouse.

She also took her hair down and brushed it, letting it fall into its natural curls around her shoulders, and freshened her makeup.

She had pitchers of sangria waiting when, one by one, her workers came over from next door. When she'd emailed everybody about the barbecue, she'd let them know they could change into fresh clothes at her place if they wanted. Those who did were directed to Tyson's bathroom upstairs, her own on the ground floor or the one in the basement apartment.

She tried not to be pleased that Derek was among the barbecue attendees—she'd been wondering if he would skip it—but she was happier than she wanted to be at the sight of him following Tyson in her back door.

She also tried not to notice how good he looked—or smelled—after disappearing upstairs for a while and then reappearing with his hair damp, his face cleanly shaven, wearing a pair of jeans that fit him to sexy perfection and a sunflower-yellow henley T-shirt that accentuated his shoulders, chest and impressively muscled biceps.

"Put me to work here, too," he commanded as Gia tore her eyes away from the sight of him and continued to put sliced pickles on the condiment tray she was preparing.

"What can I do to help?" he persisted. "I'm a great grill man if you want me to cook."

"You're a great grill man?" Gia repeated skeptically.

"Thanks to a burger joint on Colorado Boulevard where I worked when I was seventeen. You can call for references if you want."

A Camden had flipped burgers as a teenager? That was hard to believe, and Gia decided to call his bluff. "The barbecue is lit and the burgers and hot dogs are on a plate in the fridge."

"I'll need this and these—" he said, reaching into the utensil container on the counter for a spatula and tongs, as if he really did know what he was doing. Then he went to the refrigerator.

"There's veggie burgers, too, for anyone who doesn't want meat. They're on the green dish but I'll get that one—you won't be able to carry it all out."

"I think I can manage—don't stop what you're doing," he said, taking the serving platter full of hamburgers and hot dogs in one hand, and the green plate in the one that already held the tongs and spatula.

"You're sure?" Gia asked.

"Sure," he answered, pushing her screen door open with a very, very fine rear end and taking everything outside.

Gia watched him from the window above the sink, finding that he really did seem to know his way around the grill and have it all under control.

He also seemed to be a people magnet because several of her friends and coworkers migrated to the barbecue to talk while he worked.

So it isn't just me, Gia thought when she saw other people drawn to his easy manner, wit and charm.

And yet she was still jealous that other people got to be out there talking to him while she was in the kitchen....

Not only did Derek come to Gia's barbecue and man the grill, he also stayed after everyone had left to help her clean up.

"You really don't have to do this. You've done enough today and tonight," she assured him, even though she was only too happy for his company and the help—in that order.

"Come on, I'll rinse, you load the dishwasher," he answered as they finished with the backyard and headed into the kitchen that was still a mess.

"Yard work, fixing lawnmowers, painting, barbecuing, cleaning up—so much for being born with a silver spoon in your mouth, huh?" she said as he went to the sink and began to rinse the dirty dishes, handing them to her.

"I told you, my grandmother was a farm girl and we had chores. One of the other things she stuck to was that every weeknight GiGi and all ten of us kids had to meet in the kitchen to fix dinner, then eat together, then clean up. We also changed our own sheets once a week, and made our own beds before we left for school every morning. The laundry was done for us and folded, but it was set on the end of our beds for us to put away—and I mean put away, not just toss on the floor. Or else! And as soon as we were of working age and wanted more money than our allowances provided, we got jobs—summer or weekend or after school—as long as we kept our grades up. That's how I learned to be a grill man."

"So you weren't handed a Ferrari for your sixteenth birthday?" Gia said, thinking that Derek had been raised very differently from Elliot, and that while her ex hadn't received a Ferrari when he turned sixteen, he had been gifted with a sports car.

"A Ferrari when I was sixteen? How cool would that have been!" Derek said with a laugh. "Except with a car like that I probably would have been in jail or dead by the time I was sixteen and three days."

"You were not a good boy?" Gia asked as she accepted a platter from him.

"We all had our little scrapes," he answered ambiguously. "But I did run with what my grandmother considered a *fast crowd,* and that got me into some trouble—usually the girls did anyway."

"Uh-oh…" Gia said.

"Did I make it sound ominous? Because I'm not talking teenage pregnancy or anything. Just…you know… kid stuff…."

He didn't seem to want to get into the details. But not only was Gia curious, she was also eager to shut down the growing attraction she was feeling toward him, and finding out he was like Elliot growing up might help.

So she said, "You had a gang of your friends pin down a girl you didn't like in the second grade so you could beat her up? You spray-painted nasty graffiti on some-one's house and framed someone else for it and thought it was great that you got away with it while the other kid got sent to juvenile detention? You tortured some poor scrawny kid in school until the kid had a breakdown and you thought the breakdown was funny?" All things El-liot had done as a boy...which she'd learned after she'd married him.

Derek stopped midrinse to stare at her with a shocked expression. "Geez, no! I'm talking smashing pumpkins in the street on Halloween, or driving too fast, or punch-ing a friend's time card for him when he really left an hour early because *his* girlfriend had just told him she was pregnant. Or a couple of other things I got caught up in that I'm not proud of, but nothing like what you're talking about. Who did all those things? You?"

Did he seem the tiniest bit intrigued by the possibil-ity that she had?

"Me? No. I was never in any trouble."

His expression seemed to say that was what he thought and he went back to rinsing dishes. "If I'd have done even one of those things you were talking about, my grand-mother would have called me a hoodlum and she'd have lowered the boom! We didn't have the kind of perks you think we had because we were Camdens, but we did have it impressed upon us over and over that because we were Camdens we had to set a good example. That we had to step up to the plate if there was a plate that needed step-ping up to. That because we are who we are, we had to be even more above reproach than other kids. 'Eyes are always on you as a Camden,' GiGi would say."

"And she wanted you to live down the bad reputation your family name already had..." Gia said, before it oc-curred to her that maybe she shouldn't have.

But he didn't take offense.

"There was some of that. Like I told you before, GiGi thought the negative things said about us were lies, but just the fact that there were negative things said meant she wanted us to prove they were wrong. None of us would have dared to do anything like what you were talking about. Not to mention that they're really rotten and I don't think that kind of thing was in any of our natures. I don't know who you knew to even hear about stuff like that…"

Elliot Grant. Married him, didn't really know him until it was too late….

But Gia didn't say that. Instead she said, "But you *were* a hell-raiser—with the smashing pumpkins?"

"I suppose smashing Halloween pumpkins is raising hell, but it's pretty normal ornery-boy hell-raising. I went to school, made good grades—"

"And got caught up in a couple of things you aren't proud of, mostly with girls…"

He laughed. "I don't believe I said those two things together. But yes, as a matter of fact, the things I mostly got in trouble for were with girls."

And those things were…?

Gia didn't have the courage to ask that out loud, but she waited silently, hoping he would go on.

But he didn't. Instead, he handed her the last of the dishes, looked around and said, "If you tell me what you use to wash off the counters, I'll do that before I take off."

So she wasn't going to get to hear the dirt from his growing up years, and he was going to leave, too.

There was nothing good in any of that.

Still, she felt obliged to say, "You've done enough.

I'm sure you want to get home. I'll take care of the countertops."

Confirming he was worn out, he rolled his broad shoulders, arching his spine until she heard it crack, and she got to see the outline of his pectorals behind the yellow T-shirt.

Gia felt her jaw drop a fraction of an inch before she closed her mouth and swallowed. But her eyes remained glued to him as he relaxed into his normal stance and said, "Yeah, I'm starting to feel today a little."

Gia just wanted to feel him....

Those shoulders, those biceps, that chest...

She actually had to ball up her fists for a moment to fight the urge to reach across the open dishwasher door and touch him.

Then she forced her eyes away and closed the dishwasher, telling herself that she was tired and that it was bringing out weirdly primitive, primal man-woman stuff. It didn't mean anything except that he was quite a specimen of masculinity and she was woman enough not to be immune to it.

"So the yard sale next week..." Her voice wasn't as steady as it should have been, so she cleared her throat. "We can use all the donations we can get."

"Yeah, everybody in the family is gathering things to send. But after seeing this place and the Bronsons', I'm thinking that it would probably be better if I get the stuff over here Saturday morning right before your yard sale starts, because I don't know where you would store it all."

He was right—space was at a minimum.

"What we've collected so far is at the church," Gia said. "The pastor is going to bring it over on Friday night so I can price it all. So far the weather is supposed to be good, and I'm counting on that because I figure I'll keep everything under our paint tarps in the backyard until Saturday morning, then bring it out front."

"Aah, that's why you wanted to keep the paint tarps. Do you want me to bring everything over on Friday night, too?"

She did. But only so she could see him again a day sooner than she might otherwise.

Which was another urge she was determined to resist, so she said, "No, Saturday morning is fine…." Plus, if they happened to send anything more valuable than the bric-a-brac she had already accumulated, she didn't want to worry about it being outside overnight. "I can price your things then."

"I can help with that, and then I'll stick around to help run the sale with you."

"Okay…that would be nice…."

Better than nice—it suddenly made the yard sale something she was looking forward to for reasons other than the money it would raise for the Bronsons.

"But you don't have to," she added. "It doesn't take the kind of manpower the yard work and the fixes today took. I figured I could just do it myself rather than ask anybody to give up another Saturday."

"You and the minister?"

The church pastor had mentioned that he could help out. "Actually, I told him no, that just bringing the stuff over Friday night was all I needed. I didn't really want it to be just the two of us all day next Saturday—he's being kind of persistent with that going-out-with-him thing…."

And there wasn't a single thought that went through her mind in regards to the minister that even resembled what had just gone through her mind over Derek. So even if she had been willing to start dating again, it wouldn't be Pastor Brian.

Not that it would be Derek Camden, either. But still, she wished the minister would stop asking.

Derek smiled a small, knowing smile. "You sound surprised that he's so determined…."

"I just don't know why he won't give up."

"Really? You don't know why?"

"No. He must have a quota to fill for new recruits."

Derek laughed outright and furrowed his brow at her at the same time. "How long were you married?"

"Seven years."

He nodded as if that explained something. "And losing sight of your own appeal is the result of being married for seven years to a guy who didn't want to kiss you anymore…."

"I was speaking in generalities when I said that—I wasn't talking about myself," she claimed.

But it wasn't true, and she could tell by Derek's expression that he knew it.

He had the good grace not to push it, though.

He jammed his hands into his jean pockets and nodded his oh-so-handsome head in the direction of the front of her house. "I should take off—you've got to be beat, too."

"I'll walk out with you. I just realized I didn't have time to bring in the mail today."

They headed out through the archway that connected the kitchen to the living room and went to the front door.

Gia opened it and Derek held the screen door for her to go out onto the big porch with him.

"Where did you have to park?" she asked.

"A couple of doors down," he said without taking his

blue eyes off her. "But don't worry about walking me out—I think I'll be safe," he joked.

"Thanks for today…and tonight," she said then. "And for bringing in the plumbers and electricians.… You were right to think of that, since there *were* frays in the wiring. And I didn't know the toilet wasn't flushing well—the Bronsons were thrilled when I told them that had been fixed."

The elderly couple had arrived home in the middle of Gia's barbecue and she'd gone over to greet them and show them all that had been done. She'd also invited them to the barbecue, but they'd been tired after their day out and had just sent their thanks for her to convey to everyone. Even to Derek for the extra help of the professionals he'd hired.

"Both crews said things were in pretty good repair otherwise, though."

Gia nodded and once more had the fleeting thought that Derek might have something other than help up his sleeve, something that could ultimately benefit the Camdens.

But it *was* only a fleeting thought, because his gaze was still fixed on her and she wasn't sure why. She couldn't tell anything by the *way* he was looking at her, he just was. Closely. Intently. Smiling slightly.

Then his hands came to her upper arms as he leaned toward her and kissed her cheek—exactly the way a friend would.

But unlike with her friends, afterward he didn't instantly let go of her arms. Instead he went back to looking at her, looking into her eyes this time. A long, lingering look…

Go ahead…kiss me again…. she heard herself say in

her mind. And her chin tipped upward, too, because it wasn't another kiss on the cheek that she wanted.

But then Derek just squeezed her arms a little and let her go, taking the wind completely out of her sails.

"I'll be in touch," he promised as he crossed her porch and went down the four steps to the sidewalk that led out to the curb.

And then he was gone before Gia realized she hadn't said anything at all to bid him good-night.

She was just too busy responding to so many other things.

Like the feel of his big, strong hands on her arms, his fingers pressing into them, kneading them.

And that kiss…

Not the silly one on her cheek, but that other kiss that she'd so desperately wanted on her mouth that the yearning was still there.

In spite of everything…

Chapter Six

Sunday, Monday and Tuesday provided Gia with more than ample time to think about Derek, sternly reprimand herself for thinking about Derek and command herself to stop thinking about Derek. And she certainly needed to stop counting off the days that were taking her closer and closer to seeing him again.

Yet when she got a call from him on Wednesday, everything went out the window the very second she heard his voice on the other end of the line. Her pulse picked up speed and she was so happy she was nearly giddy.

And disgusted with herself for it.

Which had nothing to do with what Derek was saying, and so she also told herself to pay attention!

She realized he was telling her that he had a surprise for the Bronsons and he needed her help paving the way for them to accept it from him.

He wouldn't tell her exactly what the surprise was, he

just asked her if she could meet him at her house right after work.

Gia was disgusted with herself for telling him she would be home an hour later than she really would be in order to buy herself time to change clothes and fix her hair and makeup. But that was what she did.

Then she left work half an hour earlier than she should have in order to shower, too.

She scolded herself through the entire rush of preparations but was pleased with the end result: her hair was curly and clean; she'd applied fresh blush, mascara and lip gloss; and she was wearing her tightest jeans and a navy blue scoop-neck T-shirt over a tank top that she almost never put on because the straps were too long, exposing a hint more cleavage than she ordinarily wanted to show.

Ordinarily, but not today...

When Derek arrived, followed by a large Camden's delivery truck, her curiosity made her forget about herself and her own demons, however, and she went outside to stand on her porch.

The delivery truck parked in front of Larry and Marion's house, and Derek parked his sleek black sports car in front of her place.

She silently reprimanded herself yet again for not being able to take her eyes off him as he got out of the car. But she couldn't help devouring the sight of him. He obviously hadn't had the time to go home and change clothes because he was wearing an amazingly well-tailored tan suit over an off-white dress shirt with a brown tie. And his jaw bore a hint of scruff that was unbelievably sexy and actually made her glad he hadn't spruced up.

Plus, when he came out of his car to stand in the lee

of the open door, she got to watch him loosen the tie and slide it out from behind his collar, then open the collar button with big hands.

Next went the suit coat, which he folded in half before leaning back inside the car to drape it over the passenger seat. Then he straightened up again, unbuttoning his cuff buttons and rolling his sleeves to his elbows.

And the whole scene looked so hot to Gia that she thought he might as well have been on a stage with music playing in the background and women holding their breath waiting for him to take off more....

Well, maybe not *women,* just her....

"Hi." He greeted her with enough enthusiasm in his voice to make her wonder if he was as thrilled to see her as she was to see him.

Not that she was allowing herself to admit to being thrilled to see him....

"Hi," she answered, with some question to her tone as she nodded in the direction of the delivery truck. "*That's* the surprise?"

"What's inside is. Come on down and see," he urged, inclining his head toward the truck.

Gia went down the steps from her front porch and met him at the curb where he was waiting for her. By the time they reached the back of the delivery truck, the driver and another man had opened the rear hatch.

"I saw how old everything the Bronsons own is and I want to update them some," Derek explained. "There's a new TV—"

An enormous state-of-the-art flat screen.

"—a new couch, two recliners to replace the ones with the holes in them, and that—" he pointed to the contents on the right side of the truck "—that's an adjustable bed with a memory-foam mattress. I'm impressed with the way you have their bed rigged, but it just seemed like this might be another solution...."

A better, far more refined one. But Gia appreciated his diplomacy in not saying that.

"Will they take it all? Coming from me?" Derek asked then.

There was no doubt that the Bronsons were desperately in need of what he was offering. The stuffing was coming out of all of their furniture. Their very dated television—the only entertainment they had—was small and the picture was getting dimmer and dimmer, telling Gia that it was going to go out any minute. And the new bed was bound to make sleeping more comfortable and restful for them.

But while Larry and Marion had thawed slightly toward Derek by the time the yard work and home improvements were finished, they'd made it clear since then that their bad feelings toward the Camdens had not dissolved.

"I don't know," Gia answered honestly.

"Will they take it if we say you used some of the money you've raised to buy it all for them at cost?"

Gia couldn't take credit for something she hadn't done. Plus, she'd kept the Bronsons up-to-date on what she'd collected and how she was trying to stretch the money to meet expenses. They would know that she couldn't spend it on this.

"I can't say that, but let me talk to them. Will you wait out here?"

"As long as it takes," he said.

Gia turned and took a deep breath as she went up the Bronsons' sidewalk to their house.

The elderly couple was standing at their picture window surveying what was going on outside, and when she spotted them she smiled and waved. All the while, she was trying to decide the best tack to take on this. She couldn't use the Camdens-helping-her-help-them angle, so she decided as she went in to argue that the Camdens owed them all this.

"What's going on out there?" Larry asked when she went inside.

Gia explained the situation and then listened to their instant objections before she began her attempt to persuade them.

It took a lot, but she finally got them to agree to accept the gifts. They sat on the porch while she went in to take the bedding off their bed while Derek and his men removed the old TV and furniture and replaced them with the new.

The Bronsons' eyes were wide as they watched the men set up the TV and the top-of-the-line furniture, and got even wider as they looked over the pamphlet that told them all the functions of their new bed.

By the time the delivery men left, Larry and Marion were like two awestruck children on Christmas morning—so much so that they even relaxed their attitude toward Derek and thanked him—though not profusely.

But then they took it a step further and insisted that Derek and Gia stay for supper.

"Oh, no, I couldn't do that," Derek said, the invitation clearly taking him by surprise. "Why not let me take us all out?" he suggested, with an imploring glance at Gia that asked for her support.

She could tell just by looking at him that he was concerned about taking food from people who had so little to share. But she also knew the Bronsons, and that if they realized what he was thinking, it would embarrass them.

So she said, "You'd be sorry to miss Marion's soup and salad and homemade bread...."

"All the vegetables are from Gia's garden," Marion added, bragging about Gia. "Every bit of the salad and all but the little bit of meat I use in the broth for the soup came straight from her backyard."

"And Marion makes the noodles," Larry chimed in. "No restaurant soup can compare to that!"

"It does sound delicious..." Derek said, still looking uncertain. "If you're sure..."

"Sure, sure," Larry said.

"We just eat in the kitchen. Nothing fancy," Marion said, leading the way into that part of the house.

The meal was less awkward than Gia had feared. Derek heaped praise on Marion's cooking, which not only delighted the white-haired woman but opened the door to Larry doing some bragging of his own about the other dishes his wife made.

Derek was good about keeping the conversation light and airy, steering clear of anything that might go back too far in history and remind the Bronsons of the past ugliness between them and his family. He didn't try too hard. He just chatted and drew them out and allowed them to get comfortable with having a Camden in their kitchen with them.

"Gia, take some of the soup and a slice of bread for your lunch tomorrow," Marion decreed when they were finished eating.

"I would, but we're going out for lunch tomorrow— three of my coworkers have birthdays this week. So you guys keep it and have it for your lunch. And we're going to the Tuscan Grill—I know you like their salmon, so don't cook tomorrow night, Marion, and I'll bring you takeout from there."

"Oh, that's a treat! And we like the salmon best chilled, so it'll be cooled off by the time you get it home," Marion said.

"We couldn't do without this girl here," Larry confided in Derek. "She's always thinking about us."

"I can see that," Derek said.

Gia was uncomfortable having the attention focused on her all of a sudden, so she said to Marion, "Why don't we get these dishes done and then I'll help you make your new bed?"

"And why don't you let me show you how to operate the television, Mr. Bronson?" Derek suggested.

"Larry—he's Larry," Marion said. Then it seemed as if the words—and her own friendly overtone—surprised her, because she stopped short before she added a bit haltingly, "And I'm just Marion."

Gia waited to see if Larry would go along with the olive branch his wife had just extended. His eyes met Marion's and he smiled an understanding smile, reaching a hand over to pat hers where it rested on the table before he said to Derek, "Yep, you'd better show me what to do—tonight is the start of the new season of Marion's dancing show and she'd hate to miss that if I can't figure out how to turn the thing on."

Daylight was only beginning to wane when Gia and Derek left the Bronsons to enjoy their comfy new furniture and watch their vastly improved television.

It was a beautiful September night, and when they reached the curb in front of the Bronsons' house, rather than turning to the left where Gia's house was and where his car was parked, Derek angled his head to the right and said, "How about a walk down to Bonnie Brae for ice cream?"

Gia smiled at him. "I knew you didn't have a big, late lunch," she said, referring to the excuse he'd used for why he was eating sparingly of the soup, salad and bread. "You're still hungry."

"I felt so guilty taking food from them," he confessed. "I was afraid that whatever I ate meant they had less to eat tomorrow or the next day."

Guilt. That wasn't something she'd ever seen in Elliot.

"But sometimes they have to give a little back," she said. "It makes them feel less…needy. Sometimes you have to take what they offer, the same way you want them to take what you're offering."

"You take what they offer and then make up stories about going out to lunch the next day so you can bring them takeout to replace what you ate tonight?"

"You don't know that I'm not going out for lunch tomorrow," Gia challenged.

But he just looked at her as if he could see right through her, smiling a small smile that said yes, he did know it. "Let me buy you ice cream—you didn't eat any more than I did."

There was no question that she should say no. But when she opened her mouth, "I never turn down ice cream" came out, and they headed toward the creamery walking side by side.

"Do you do as much for your own family as you do for the Bronsons?" Derek asked her then.

"I would if I had a family to do for," she answered.

"Oh, that's right—I think you told me that. That the Bronsons have become family for you, that you don't have any family of your own, right?"

"I might have a father out there somewhere, but he left my mother and me when I was seven and no one ever heard from him again, so I don't really know if he's still living or not."

"He just took off?"

"Just took off," she confirmed. "He'd been telling my mother how he'd made a mistake to get married and have a kid, that it had shown him that he wanted a different life than that. My mother tried to make it work, tried to figure out how he could have what he wanted and us, too, but the truth was that he just didn't want us. One day he went to work and never came home. When she looked for him, she found out he hadn't gone to work at all. He'd used the day to empty their bank account, clear out every other asset they had, cash his last paycheck and leave town—"

"Without so much as saying goodbye?" Derek asked in amazement.

"Without a word."

"And that was it? You never heard from him again? Not a card or a letter or a phone call?"

"Nothing. He'd talked about traveling, about not wanting to live in Colorado anymore, so my mom didn't have a doubt that he'd left the state, but beyond that…" Gia shrugged. It had all happened so long ago that the wounds she'd nursed through childhood had healed. "I have no idea what happened to him."

"Ever thought of looking for him?"

She shook her head. "When I was a kid I had fantasies—he'd come home, say what a mistake he'd made and we'd all live happily ever after. But when I grew out of those… No, I wouldn't look for him. I can understand people who are adopted and hope that they'll find their biological parents and learn that the reason they were given up was just because there was no other way, that it was what was best for them or it wouldn't have been done. But for me… My father spent seven years with me and then…" Okay, maybe there were still some old wounds, because her voice cracked unexpectedly.

She cleared her throat. "He made it pretty clear that he didn't want anything to do with me. It wasn't even a matter of him divorcing my mom, He could have made sure he was still in my life in some way—even long-distance. But he wanted out and he got out. And he didn't leave us a thing, so he obviously didn't care what happened to us—not whether we had a roof over our heads or food to eat or clothes on our backs. That only says bad things about him as a human being, as a man. Why would I go looking for someone like that?"

They'd arrived at the ice cream shop by then and were lucky not to find a line out the door.

As they went up to the display freezers, Derek said, "Chocolate, right? It's just a matter of how dark or what extras might be in it."

"Actually, I like vanilla ice cream."

He laughed. "You're kidding?"

"Really rich, creamy vanilla. With little specks of vanilla bean in it and nothing else. On a wafer cone, not a sugar cone—they're too sweet for me."

"Okay," he said with another laugh, conceding to the unexpected. "When it comes to ice cream, I *do* like chocolate."

"Then there's hope for you yet," Gia teased him.

He laughed once more, as if he hadn't expected that, either. "I'm not sure what that means—was there no hope for me before?" Just then, the girl behind the counter came to take their order, freeing Gia from having to answer that.

When they had their ice cream cones, Gia and Derek sat down at the one unoccupied café table outside.

"So what happened after your father left?" Derek asked when they were sitting contentedly eating ice cream. "Were you and your mom okay? Was there *only* you and your mom, or have you lost siblings along the way, too?"

"I was an only child. And things were rough after my father left. My mom had a lot of health problems— a bad valve in her heart, some immune-system things, bad digestive issues—so she hadn't been working, and the stress of my father leaving made her sicker. We had to move in with my grandparents, who really did more of the parenting than my mom did because she was just too sick. She died when I was eleven, and I just went on with Gramma and Grampa."

"So you were raised by grandparents, too."

"I was. And they were great. They spoiled me rotten, but who's going to complain about that? I loved them dearly."

"But they're not around anymore?" he asked cautiously.

"They were killed in a car accident caused by a drunk driver just before I graduated from college...." Another lump in her throat paused what she was saying and kept her from eating ice cream for a moment. Then she blinked back the tears that came with the memory and went on.

"I didn't go through the graduation ceremony because they weren't there to see it—it felt so bad to finish the education they'd paid for and not have them around for the grand finale." And then she'd leaped into marriage to fill the gap—not only with Elliot and the possibility of a family of her own, but also thinking that the big, close-knit Grant family would embrace her and take the place of her grandparents.

Grief-clouded reasoning…

"Wow, I'm doing a lot of talking about myself tonight," she said in a lighter vein.

But he must not have minded, because he stuck to the topic. "So it seems like the Bronsons are replacement grandparents for you. But you didn't have them until three years ago, when you were going through *another* tough time…."

"Divorce that round. My marriage came out of losing my grandparents and finding myself with no one— except Tyson, but you know, no family—and Larry and Marion came out of the divorce. They're a much better deal," she joked.

Looking perplexed by that, he part smiled, part frowned. "Two eighty-plus-year-olds in hard times are a better deal than your marriage was?"

"Believe it or not," she said with a laugh of her own. But she didn't offer more than that because she really did feel as if she'd been talking about herself for too long.

And since they'd finished their ice cream, she also didn't think she should draw out her time with Derek more than she already had, because it worried her how much she wanted to.

"I should get home," she said then. "I'm harvesting in Broomfield all day tomorrow, so I have to leave here a lot earlier in the morning."

He gave her a slow, victorious smile. "The Tuscan Grill is in Cherry Creek—that's a long way from Broomfield," he said, calling her on her subterfuge.

Gia made a face and laughed at the same time. "Oh, yeah…"

"What are you going to do, order the takeout on your

way back from Broomfield and pick it up before you go home?"

She merely shrugged as they stood and started back toward her house. "Shh...don't give away my secrets."

"Will the salmon be cooled off enough to cover your tracks?"

"I'll come home, put it in my fridge while I shower and then bring it to them."

"So you're a little sneaky," he teased.

"Only when I have to be, and for a good cause."

"I'll bet," he said as if she were predictable that way.

And somehow that made her feel a little boring....

"Is there anything I can do for Saturday's yard sale besides bring stuff over in the morning and work it with you?" he asked then. "Do you need help tagging things or setting up or—"

"Thanks, but I have it under control." She wished she could say the same about her responses to him.

Because she'd been overly aware of every tiny detail since watching him get out of his car earlier.

Because each and every time she so much as glanced at him something tingly went off inside her.

Because there was a part of her that kept willing him to take her hand or her arm, to touch her some way, any way.

Because just walking along the sidewalk with him was so nice that she was keeping her pace ultraslow in order to prolong it.

And all of that was out of control....

"Minna left Sunday for Reno to visit her parents and didn't get back until today, so Tyson and I have been going over to the church in the evenings to mark and organize things," she added. "We have almost everything ready, so Friday night I'll just be directing traffic when the church group gets it all here," she explained, sticking to her resolution to resist having him come then.

"You and Tyson…" Derek said then. "You're just friends, huh?"

Even the faintest suspicion that they were more than that made her laugh. "Just friends," she confirmed. "Since we were both seven—"

"When your dad left."

"And when Mom and I moved in with my grandparents. Tyson and his family had just moved into the house behind theirs."

"Did you go to school together?"

"We did."

"But you never hooked up as boyfriend and girlfriend?"

Gia laughed again. "We were *seven* when we met. I've seen him do yucky, disgusting kid things. We had chicken pox together, we've gone through bad skin, braces, the worst of puberty, getting drunk at thirteen on stolen liquor at a wedding and throwing up in matching trash cans. I think we've just never had enough illusions about each other to be anything *but* friends."

"You think people need to have some illusions to be something other than friends?"

Gia shrugged again as they reached her house and she stopped by his car. "I just think people *do* have illusions about the people they get involved with as more than friends. They probably *shouldn't,* but attraction seems to put on blinders and narrow your vision."

"Are we talking about your marriage again?" he asked.

Rather than answer that, Gia said, "Were your eyes wide-open right from the start with Tyson's cousin, Sharon-the-wannabe-psychic?"

He smiled a slow smile, conceding her point. "Attraction makes you overlook anything *except* what you're attracted to. Then, later on, what you overlooked—or missed altogether because of the blinders—is what makes the relationship not work…."

"Exactly," she said.

He nodded toward her house. "Can I walk you up?" he offered.

"No, I'm fine—the porch light is on, you can see no one is lurking in the bushes waiting for me…."

He actually took a glance around to make sure, but he didn't insist.

He also didn't make any move to go around to the driver's side of his car, staying where he was and looking down at her much the way he had when he'd left on Saturday night.

Just before he'd given her that friendly kiss that had been sooo disappointing….

"I guess I have fewer illusions about you after tonight," he joked then, returning to their conversation. "Chocolate everything except ice cream—very strange. Sneaky when it's called for and for a good cause. And you wore braces and got drunk at thirteen…."

"And I talk too much if you let me," she added.

"You only answered my questions. Most of them…" he said, likely referring to what she hadn't said about her marriage.

But the way he was looking at her and the small smile that curved just the corners of his mouth made her think that there wasn't anything about what he'd learned tonight that he didn't like.

And no matter how much she wished she would have discovered something about him that *she* didn't like, she hadn't yet….

Then, just when she was looking up into that handsome face and those shockingly blue eyes and starting to think about kissing again, he must have read her mind, because he said, "How about kissing—did you and Tyson try that out together the first time just for the sake of experimentation or for practice?"

"No," she said as if that was unimaginable. "I wouldn't have kissed a brother if I'd had one, and Tyson is like that to me."

Derek's smile grew. "I don't know why I'm so glad to hear that," he said, his eyes staying on hers.

And staying and staying…

While something seemed to swirl in the air around them, making Gia wonder if they'd been standing that close together the whole time or if they'd somehow moved closer.

Close enough so that he didn't even have to touch her. He just leaned over enough to kiss her—this time not on the cheek like any friend might, but on the lips.

And oh, but that was so, so much better than the kiss on the cheek!

Because he was so, so good at it!

His lips were warm and just right—parted just the right amount, not too dry, not too wet, just a little sweet. And he let the kiss go on long enough for her to kiss him back, all with that indescribable something in the atmosphere around them, making where they were, who they were and everything else feel as if they were somewhere outside of time, protected from it all.…

But just when she was drifting away on that kiss, it ended.

Long before she wanted it to.…

And he went back to looking down into her eyes for a moment until he said, "I'll see you Saturday morning."

Gia nodded, working to find her voice. "I'll be putting things out by seven and there'll be coffee."

"I'll need a lot of it at seven. See, one less illusion about me—I'm not a morning person."

"Me, neither," she confessed.

"Good," he said, as he turned and went around his car to unlock his door, adding with a second nod at her house, "Go on. If you won't let me walk you up, I at least need to see from here that you're inside."

Following orders, she went up the walkway to her porch, slipping her house key out of her pocket so she could unlock her door when she reached it.

Then she went inside, turned, waved and called, "Safe!"

He smiled, waved back and got behind the wheel.

Leaving Gia to wonder what in the world was going on between them.

And knowing that she shouldn't be letting it....

Chapter Seven

"Thanks for the help," Derek said to Louie Haliburton.

It was late Friday night and Derek and Louie had just finished loading Louie's truck with items for Gia's yard sale on Saturday. They were in the garage of the Camden family home, where the truck would stay until Derek picked it up in the morning.

Louie accepted the open beer Derek had gone into the house for and sat on a stack of boxes to drink it. "Thanks," he said.

Derek sat on the steps that led to the kitchen. "No, thank you for the help," he countered, taking a long pull of his own beer before leaning forward to brace his elbows on his knees, holding the bottle between them.

"This is all for somebody's yard sale?" Louie asked, even though he knew the answer because Derek had told him. "You're helping out some old couple with problems?"

"Yeah. There were donation jars around for the same cause—you probably saw them…. Couple's name is Bronson…"

"Yeah, I did see those. That what got you involved?"

"That and they're members of a church that one of GiGi's friends belongs to, so she wanted us to help out," Derek said, telling a partial truth to cover the real reason.

"And this Gia you've been talking about all night is behind it?"

"Have I been talking about her all night?" Derek was aware of always thinking about her—that had been going on since he'd met her and he couldn't seem to stop it. But he'd mentioned her to Louie, too? Without even realizing it? And a noteworthy amount?

Strange.

"Her name's been about every other word you've said tonight," Louie went on. "Gia this. Gia that. Gia says this, does that, thinks this or that. You'll ask Gia about some natural remedy for Margaret's allergies and for the wart on my finger because she's some kind of plant scientist or something."

Derek chuckled. "A botanist. For a company that makes supplements and natural remedies for things," he clarified, before adding, "Sorry, I didn't realize how much I was talking about her."

"She sounds like a nice girl. I'm surprised you like her."

"Who said I like her?"

Louie merely gave him a look over his beer bottle as the older man took a drink.

"I don't…you know…*like* her like I'm interested in her," Derek protested.

"Sound pretty interested to me…"

Hard to deny when he'd apparently talked about her

all night. When he knew how she was on his mind constantly. When twice he had ignored every warning in his head and kissed her....

"I'm trying to take a breather from women," Derek said.

Trying to...

Before he'd met Gia he'd been *determined* to....

"After Vegas, you know..." he added, not eager to say more than that.

"Turning point," Louie summed up. "Should have been."

A man of few words that still managed to pack a punch.

"Yeah...I know," Derek agreed. And he *did* agree with Louie. And the rest of his family, who all held the same opinion. "I'm just not sure I *can* turn over a new leaf with women," he confided in the man he'd been going to for advice since he was a boy. "You're attracted to who you're attracted to, you know?"

"I know that if you keep doing what you've always done, you're going to keep getting what you've got—"

"Nothing. But trouble." And a whole heaping of embarrassment this time around.

"You're always saying that the regular girls don't keep your interest, but seems to me like the strange ones don't, either..." Louie observed as he raised his bottle to take another drink.

"I never thought of it that way," Derek admitted.

"You haven't ended up with any of them."

"Because either strange gets annoying or *too* strange, or because I'm not weird enough to keep *their* interest."

"Seems like a flawed system."

Derek laughed. "Yeah, so far. But you have to admit,"

he defended himself, "a little wild is fun. It keeps you guessing."

"You just guessed wrong in Vegas?" Louie said before he took another drink of his beer.

Derek flinched.

"Wild is one thing," the older man went on then. "You can put a little wild in anything. Weird is something else. And conniving and devious and scheming that come out of the weird—those are just bad."

"I can't argue with that," Derek muttered. Then he gave the older man a look out of the corner of his eye and an insinuating smile. "So that's the secret of marriages that last—you just add a little wild?"

Louie merely smiled, not taking the bait to tell stories out of school, and finishing his beer instead.

Then he stood and went to the recycle bin. "If you find the right person, it all works out. Everything you need, everything you want is there. But like I said, keep doing what you've been doing, you'll keep getting what you've got."

The challenge came with the clink of the bottle going into the bin, and Derek was reasonably sure that was meant to reinforce the message.

Then Louie headed to where Derek was sitting, patting him on the shoulder to soften the exchange as he climbed the steps past Derek and went into the kitchen, leaving Derek in the garage alone.

And thinking about Gia again.

The way he always seemed to be lately.

Gia was definitely a veer from the norm for him, that was for sure. She was a Girl Scout through and through, someone without any edge at all that he'd been able to find.

But he still liked her. He was still interested in her.

He wasn't sure why, but he was, and after kissing her on Wednesday night it was pretty clear that he was failing at laying low for a while when it came to women.

But since she *was* a Girl Scout and he hadn't yet lost interest in her, maybe he should ride this out and see where it went, he thought. Explore it a little.

Carefully, though.

He didn't want to hurt her.

He wouldn't hurt her for anything in the world. It would be a crime with someone like her.

So he had to be careful in case his attraction to her was only a subconscious overcompensation for the fiasco of Vegas—a sharp recoil from that to someone who was the exact opposite.

Because if that was the case, when the fog had lifted, he might not be so infatuated with Gia. He might return to his old pattern and lose interest.

But the fact was, he *had* found some appeal in Gia, and he couldn't deny it.

Hell, he couldn't resist it.

No matter how hard he tried.

Gia's yard sale was a success. There was virtually nothing left by the end of it.

But after marking and organizing everything until well after midnight on Friday night and then getting out of bed at 5:00 a.m. Saturday morning to set up, when it was finally time to call it a day, Gia was dragging.

Seeing her exhaustion, Derek insisted that she come to his house for a pampering dinner as a reward for all her hard work.

Well, maybe he hadn't *insisted.* He'd invited and coaxed. But as Gia showered and got ready, she told herself that he'd insisted and that she was too worn-out to put up much of a fight. So she'd accepted the offer for those reasons, not because an entire day with him hadn't seemed like enough or because she just couldn't deny herself the chance to see his place and spend a little more time with him.

Besides, she argued with herself after showering, shampooing, scrunching her hair, applying makeup and agonizing over what to wear, today was the last of the fund-raising efforts on the Bronsons' behalf. From here on, she wasn't sure what Derek's involvement might or might not include. A phone call here and there just to check on the Bronsons' evolving situation? An occasional drop by?

One way or another, she was reasonably sure she wouldn't be spending entire days with him the way she had been. And while that thought did not sit well, she didn't want to analyze why, so instead she merely decided that one more evening with him couldn't do any harm.

So, dressed in a pair of black cigarette pants and a flowy white lace top over a tank that fitted her like a second skin, she drove the short distance from her house to his in the heart of one of Cherry Creek's most coveted gated communities.

His house was a sprawling gray-brick ranch built in an L shape around a stone drive that led to a four-car garage.

"Wow! This is *not* what I expected," Gia said as he let her in the oversize front door and she stepped into a traditionally furnished space that was homey despite its size.

"What did you expect?"

"Fraternity house chic? *Playboy* mansion? Snake aquariums—"

"Snake aquariums?"

"You sort of have a reputation…. Tyson says one of Sharon's friends who you dated after her was big on snakes, so I thought maybe—"

"No, no snake aquariums for me. I like snakes, but not when you wake up in the middle of the night and find that one has gotten out and into bed with you—"

"Eww!" Gia said in horror.

He laughed. "Yeah, can't say I was thrilled. So no, no snakes. You can relax."

But as he led her through the expansive entrance to a great room and very impressive kitchen she continued to find the house surprisingly cozy. It had the air of a place that was built for a large family.

"No snakes, but are you sure your wife and half dozen kids aren't coming out any minute?" she said, taking in the sight of the kitchen with its six-burner gas stove and built-in grill, the double ovens, more cupboards than she would know what to do with, the island with its eight bar stools and the dining table not far from it with seats for twelve.

"*Annulled,* remember? So no wife. And no kids anywhere, either," he assured her.

"You just rattle around this big place by yourself?"

"I do. I was looking for a house when it came on the market and it was such a good buy—almost fully furnished, and I even liked the furniture—so I decided to go for it even if it is more house than I need right now. I figure someday I won't be the only one here. And I come from a big family—having poker night or a movie night or a dinner calls for—" he waved a hand negligently in the air "—all this."

Right…

Big family.

Big, close-knit family.

With a history of doing things that weren't nice.

It was a reminder for her.

A warning that she needed to not be distracted by the fact that he looked fabulous freshly showered, wearing jeans that perfectly skimmed a fantastic derriere and thick thighs, and a gray mock-neck T-shirt that caressed every muscle of impressive shoulders, pecs and biceps.

And he smelled good, too....

"It's beautiful," she said about the house, wishing he was less attractive himself.

"Thanks. I thought we'd eat French tonight—there's a new bistro that I heard was good and they deliver. Delivered—about ten minutes ago. I set us up outside. I'm trying to get every last minute I can on the patio before the weather turns and it gets too cold. There's French wine waiting out there for us, too."

He leaned close and confided, "And for dessert they have what I'm told is a remarkably dark chocolate cake with twelve thin layers of cake separated by ganache— I'm not quite sure how that's different from frosting, but I guess it is."

"Frosting has confectioner's sugar. Ganache is just chocolate and cream," she explained.

"And your eyes get a special sparkle just saying it," he observed, laughing. "I also got a crème brûlée—maybe we can share. Although I promise not to eat a full half of your cake, maybe just a bite or two."

"Good, because crème brûlée does nothing for me," she joked.

"The patio is out this way," he directed, ushering her past an entertainment center with a nearly theater-size television at its heart and through sliding doors to his backyard.

Unlike the rest of the house, the yard was not massive. In fact, it was smaller than Gia's and taken up primarily with a stone-paved patio surrounded by a tiered rock garden.

It was equally as beautiful as the house, though, and she told him so. "You just need some greenery and some flowers planted around the rocks for color—all you have is moss."

"Maybe I can be your next project…" he said in a way she didn't take seriously.

There was a waterfall within the rocks, and one of the three patio tables he had was positioned right in front of it. The table was set for two, complete with plates, napkins, silverware, wine and wineglasses. Sitting on another table not far away was a paper bag with the bistro's logo stamped on it.

As he held out a chair for her and she took it, he said, "We have two steaks au poivre, asparagus, baby fingerling parsley-butter potatoes and bread to tear and smear with whipped butter before we can get to dessert—sound okay?"

"It sounds like heaven—I'm starving!"

"You should be," he said, retrieving the bag from the other table once she was seated. "I don't think you took more than two bites of your lunch between customers today."

Customers who had mostly been people Gia and the Bronsons knew, so they'd wanted to chat, too. So no, Gia hadn't had more than a scant taste of lunch.

"The Bronsons seemed to enjoy it all," he said as he poured wine. "I don't think either of them went inside or sat down for five minutes today, they were so busy talking to people. They had to be worn-out."

"They were. By the time I left them they had TV trays set up, and were eating the pizza I talked them into having delivered so Marion wouldn't need to cook. They also had popcorn and their movie ready to watch."

"Good for them," Derek said as he took food from containers and arranged it on each of their plates like a pro.

He sat down then and raised his glass. "To you—for all the work you did for them."

Gia laughed uncomfortably. "Oh, dear. I don't think anyone has ever toasted me before. I'm not exactly sure what to say to that."

"How about you just have a sip of wine and we eat?" he suggested.

She agreed to that and sipped the red wine, which was smooth and dry. "Oh, those French!" she said when she'd also tasted her food. "They know their stuff!"

"We weren't led astray," Derek agreed before he said, "So how did you do—today and on the whole?"

"For the Bronsons?"

He nodded because his mouth was full.

"Today surprised me," she admitted. "I've never had a yard sale or a garage sale where pretty much everything sold. And mostly without any bickering over the price. I think it was just because of where the money was going—everybody wanted to do what they could for Larry and Marion, so they bought something."

"Did it put you over the top for them?"

Gia made a face as she chewed a spear of asparagus. "It helped," she hedged when she could talk. "I should be able to pay a fair share of the past-due payments. Not quite all of it, but I think I have enough to put us in a position to negotiate with the bank—"

"Always negotiate," he advised, listening intently as he ate.

"I'm hoping the bank will take what I have and either

forgive the rest or refinance. *If* I can refinance. And if I can, then there's the new payments—I'm not sure I'll be able to get them low enough for the Bronsons to keep up on them. Then, depending on what comes out of it all, I'll have to talk to Larry and Marion and we'll see…"

"So the house is still in jeopardy," he summed up.

"A little bit less imminent jeopardy, because I should be able to pay the bank enough to stall foreclosure, but yes. And we have to face the fact that rallying everybody, getting donations, fixing everything up, was a one-time thing. If it looks as if Larry and Marion could end up where they are again in a year or two, because even the payments on a refinance are too high, then they're better off selling now while things are shipshape."

"And moving into your basement."

"They'll still have their new furniture and TV and bed…" she pointed out, to let him know that his gifts would not go to waste.

He nodded that handsome head of his but didn't comment. Instead he said, "Well, all I can say is that anybody in trouble should have you in their corner."

Again Gia wasn't comfortable with the praise, so she deflected it. "You brought a lot to the table that I wouldn't have been able to accomplish or give them," Gia said. "I appreciate that."

Which was true.

"So we'll just take it from here," he said.

She wasn't sure what that meant and felt uncomfortable asking because she didn't want to seem avaricious, even on the Bronsons' behalf. So she just let that hang and said, "I also appreciate this food—it's great!"

"It is, isn't it? This place should be around for a while."

"I'm stuffed, though," Gia added, pushing away her plate.

"Too stuffed for dessert?" he challenged, having finished his own meal.

"Oh, I have a special stomach compartment for that," she joked.

He laughed again. "Why don't I doubt that? But how about if we hold off long enough for me to clear, maybe make some coffee to go with the dessert.... I can make espresso if you like your coffee as dark as your chocolate."

"I do, actually. But I never drink it this late or I'll be up all night—"

And why did that get an arch of one eyebrow from him as if that was a tempting idea?

Maybe she was imagining it, because it was gone again a split-second later and all he said was, "So no coffee. More wine, then?"

"Maybe just a quarter of a glass—it might not be far, but I still have to drive home...and I'll help clean up," she said, standing when he did.

"Nooo," he overruled. "This was to pamper and reward you, remember? You sit over there—" he pointed to a built-in, cushioned seating area next to the waterfall "—and I'll clear this stuff and be right back."

Gia tried arguing with him, but he took her by the shoulders, guided her to where he wanted her to sit and pressured her to sit there.

In the few minutes he was gone she caught herself relishing the way it had felt to have those big, strong hands on her shoulders and tried to shake off the pleasure she'd found in it.

The view of the sun setting over the rock garden and the waterfall was spectacular, so Gia focused on that in the hopes of gaining some perspective until Derek reappeared, bringing their desserts.

He sat beside her and poured them both just a little more wine. Then he angled toward her and they tasted both the cake and the crème brûlée.

"Okay, this time I like the chocolate better, too," he admitted.

"I'll share," she offered, but he merely laughed at that, propped an ankle on the opposite knee and settled in to eat the sugar-crusted custard.

Lights automatically turned on around them then, and Gia only hoped she looked as good in soft glow as he did.

"I keep wondering," he said then, "what do I 'sort of have a reputation' for?"

It was what she'd said when she'd first arrived.

Gia shrugged, unsure if she should say.

But despite the fact that she never felt as if she had enough time with him, they *had* been together frequently, for hours and hours on end, and that had established a relaxed air between them. Out of that had come more and more openness, more and more honesty, more and more teasing and giving each other a hard time. And it also allowed her to feel as if she could answer him honestly.

Plus, she *was* curious about his past and this seemed like a route to finding out about it.

So she said, "Well, there was Sharon—the *psychic*. And Tyson heard through Sharon that after her you dated two people you met when you were with her—friends of hers. The one with the snakes and another one who Tyson says was weird, too—something about performance art…."

"When I was with her she was into making herself look like a statue of a Greek goddess and then standing on the street fooling people into thinking she really was a statue. It was pretty amazing to see, actually—you couldn't even catch her breathing or blinking. The trouble was that even when she wasn't all made up and in costume she liked to spontaneously freeze and go into the act—walking in the mall, sitting in a restaurant, with my family... And when she did it, she wouldn't stop doing it and come back to life until she felt like it."

"How long would that take?"

"I never knew—that was part of the problem. I could just be walking along, talking to her, and *bam!* I'd look over and she was gone. Then I'd find her six feet behind me where she'd stopped in her tracks. And no matter how inconvenient it was or how much anyone tried to get her out of it, she wouldn't. She sat through an entire Sunday dinner at my grandmother's in statue mode. It got to be like dating someone who went catatonic without warning and I just had to wait until she came to again."

Gia tried to suppress a smile but failed. "So *three* off-the-wall girlfriends—"

"I don't know that you'd call all of them *girlfriends*—mostly it was just dating."

But he'd apparently slept with the snake charmer, if one of her snakes had slithered into bed with him....

"That Sunday dinner was the end for Theresa," he said, interrupting Gia's wandering thoughts. "And I'd been seeing her less than a month then."

"Well, that's where your reputation came from. With Tyson and me. Maybe you just had a brief streak of strange and out of that we unfairly labeled you."

Wishful thinking?

"Ah, if only I could say it was just a streak of strange..." he said with a laugh.

"You earned the reputation we gave you with more than the three?"

"I do tend toward women who are a little different..." he confessed.

"Different..." she repeated.

"Unique...with an edge. Sometimes too much of an edge...."

"Bad girls?"

"Sometimes... My first crush in second grade was on Molly Ryker—she drew what the teacher called *very naughty* pictures on the back of the girl who sat in front of her. Watching her do it..." He inclined his head. "I was hooked."

"You liked the danger?" Gia asked, knowing that she certainly couldn't be considered dangerous.

"I think what I liked with Molly was the fearlessness. And that's—I don't know—kind of a theme. Bold. Strong. Determined. Dedicated. Women who push boundaries, challenge things. Women with a passion for something. Women who just have an extra element. Who are...let's say, colorful. It's been a pattern with me." He shook his head and laughed as if it had begun to confuse him in some way. "They're just more interesting...."

"And interesting to you is over-the-top bad girls."

"Over-the-top has, in the past, helped keep me around for a while longer than run-of-the-mill," he confirmed. "But bad girls have gotten me into trouble...."

"Into trouble...and an annulled marriage?"

"And an annulled marriage," he echoed in a more ominous tone than Gia had said it.

"So there are two categories. There's weird—like Sharon-the-wannabe-psychic and her friends—"

"And there was one who excused herself during Sunday dinner, went into the bathroom and shaved her head just to shock everybody. And there was the one who was heavily tattooed and pierced. And there was a Goth—"

Gia smiled and couldn't resist goading. "You drank blood and slept in a coffin with that one?"

He laughed and took her teasing in stride. "I would never drink blood, and I didn't sleep with her so I don't know if there was a coffin involved. There's also been more than one into extreme diet things—they either drove my grandmother crazy trying to feed us their recipes at Sunday dinner or there was one who wanted to play food police and tell everybody what they could and couldn't eat. And there was one who was into obscure religions—the screechy chanting eventually got to me—"

"Do it," Gia encouraged, again giving him a hard time.

He laughed. "I value my relationship with my neighbors, so no."

"And those were only the weird ones? Those weren't the bad girls who led you to get an annulment?"

He flinched, and she could tell it was a sore enough subject that she needed to be more careful about it.

"Those were the *colorful* ones," he amended. "But no, they weren't the bad girls who got me into real trouble."

"So what did the bad girls do?" she asked, hating herself for wondering so much what it was he found interesting.

His expression made it clear that he wasn't proud of what he was about to say. "I was brought into police custody after my tenth-grade girlfriend took me for a joyride in a car I didn't know was stolen. There was an actual arrest—me and about a hundred other kids got caught trespassing when we went to a party another girlfriend threw at a house she'd broken into that I didn't *know* she'd broken into. And there was an incident with a girl in college who took a picture of me from behind and sold copies of it for fun and profit. That was bad enough, but the picture got into a newspaper article about college campuses gone wild—"

"A *naked* picture?"

"'Fraid so…"

Gia wished she'd seen it.…

But she didn't say that. Instead, as they both set their dessert dishes aside and she turned to face him, pulling her legs up underneath her, she said more gingerly, "And then there was the annulment, too.…"

Derek took a deep breath, exhaled sharply and said, "*That* came out of a trip to Las Vegas this past spring— so I didn't have the excuse of being young and clueless. I went for a bachelor party and I met a woman—"

"Who you liked because she was either weird or a bad girl."

"She was the bartender at the party and she just seemed like fun."

"Which, for you, means something about her was over-the-top or edgy."

"It didn't seem like that, no. She was just funny, clever, quick, and that made her fun to talk to, so I spent a lot of time standing at the bar talking to her. Unfortunately, that led to getting really, *really* drunk. I know the party went on into the early-morning hours, and then I left with her.…" He shook his head. "Things are fuzzy after that…but apparently Krista and I ended up taking a walk through a drive-in wedding chapel, where I guess I got married.…"

"You don't remember it at all?"

"Not at all. But there are pictures and a certificate— proof that it happened."

"Was the bartender drunk, too?"

"Oh, I think she was perfectly sober," he said. "I think

Krista basically set a trap when she'd figured out who I was, and I just fell into it. And once I had, she had those pictures and that marriage certificate to hold for ransom...."

"Did she want to stay married to you?" Gia asked, because that didn't seem beyond the realm of possibility to her. This was Derek after all. The man sitting near enough for her to smell the scent of his woodsy cologne, for her to see his strikingly handsome face awash in golden light, for her to know firsthand how appealing he was.

"No, she didn't want to stay married to me," he said wryly. "What she wanted was a boatload of money— that's what it cost three days later to persuade her to agree to the annulment."

"If you didn't pay..."

"She wouldn't let the marriage be annulled. She said she'd wait awhile and then sue me for divorce and breach of promise. The lawyers thought the annulment would be the cheaper route, so—"

"You gave her the boatload of money."

"And got the annulment. Then that wasn't enough. Even though my attorneys had her sign a gag order, her friend—who had witnessed the ceremony and taken the pictures—blogged about it and the whole thing went public anyway—"

"Oh, that's awful. And a rotten thing to do!" Gia said sympathetically.

"Yeah. But...who we are—the Camden name and position—means we have to be especially careful. There are people out there like Krista—and her friend—and if we do something stupid and give them an open door..." He shook his head in what looked like self-disgust. "I haven't paid enough attention to that. But this was the worst yet. The worst embarrassment because it couldn't be written off as teenage stupidity or a college prank. And to have our name thrown around that publicly... I made us a laughingstock. Not a proud moment. Everybody ended up answering for my dumbass mistake...."

It was obvious that he took the blame and was not only embarrassed himself, but ashamed, too, and Gia wasn't sure what to say. She settled on, "It seems like you've learned a lesson."

He laughed humorlessly. "That's what everybody is hoping."

"But you aren't sure?"

"I'm trying to lay low. Change my pattern. Turn over a new leaf. But...I don't know... My family is always trying to find me a *regular* girl—that's what they call them. But somehow the *regular* girls they fix me up with either bore me to tears or...I guess I'm the king of losing interest. And then there I am, back again finding someone more...colorful."

"Tattooed, pierced, chanting, head-shaving, dirt-eating, snake-charming psychics," she concluded.

He laughed and Gia was glad to see that she'd been able to lift his spirits. "Who said anybody ate dirt?"

"Food police, dirt eating—it just seemed possible for you."

He chuckled again, shaking his head at her summary and looking more intently at her.

She had the sense that injecting some humor had helped to draw him out of himself, that he wasn't lost in his own demons any longer, because there was a renewed sparkle to his oh-so-blue eyes as his smile turned slightly wicked.

Which Gia knew meant that he had a comeback for her.

"So I guess somewhere under that good-girl exterior

of yours must be a little evil, since the curse of the *regular* girl never seems to kick in when it comes to you.... What's your secret, Grant? Maybe you're the dirt eater?"

Gia laughed. "It's the real reason I became a botanist— when I'm potting plants I just stuff myself with handfuls of it."

"I knew it!" he said in mock victory. "I knew there had to be something!"

"And there it is—my deepest, darkest secret..." she said, playing along.

He narrowed his gorgeous eyes at her and leaned in slightly closer to look into hers. "You may not eat dirt, but there's still a little evil in there.... You aren't fooling me...I see it," he said suspiciously.

Gia just smiled, terrified by how much she liked him and unable to curb it even when she tried.

Then he closed the gap between them to kiss her.

It didn't take any more than that for her to stop trying completely. To give in to what she seemed to want all the time now. To just be kissed by him. To just kiss him back.

His left hand sluiced under her hair to the back of her head to brace her. When his lips parted, so did hers as she let her head rest in that cradle.

He took her hand in his, holding it, rubbing it with his thumb as she got her first introduction to his tongue.

Inviting and enticing and persuasive, he coaxed her to play and Gia did, volleying and toying and fencing right along with him.

There was just something about him....

Every texture, every taste, every nuance was exactly right. Exactly what she wanted, exactly when she wanted it.

He used her hand to pull her nearer. Then he laid it

to his chest and let go of it so he could wrap his arm around her.

It was almost strange how well she fit there. So well she just wanted to burrow into him as her palm absorbed the heat of his body and the hardness of his pectorals to add to pleasures that seemed to be mounting by the minute.

Pleasures that still centered on their mouths that were locked together, sealed in kissing fueled by more kissing, by tongues that frolicked with each other.

Gia was faintly aware of the sounds of the waterfall nearby, but it only seemed to carry her along, to draw her even more serenely into kissing Derek, into being kissed by him so thoroughly that she felt like it was all she would ever need. Kissing him and kissing him. Being held in his strong arms, against his broad chest now, with her hand the only thing keeping them from coming together seamlessly.

She had no idea how much time passed while they were making out. At some point it occurred to her that it had been a very long time, and that it was late because even through her closed eyes she could tell that the moon had gotten high in the sky to add a brighter, whiter glow to the golden illumination of the patio lights.

She needed to stop this, she told herself. To go home. To talk some sense into herself....

As much as she really, really didn't want to, she knew she had to. So her tongue became a little shy, a little more difficult to catch, and she pushed against the stone wall of Derek's chest and drew back almost imperceptibly.

He didn't want to let her go, because he only held her tighter, kissed her more thoroughly.

But just long enough to convey his reluctance before he conceded to the message she'd given, ending that kiss only to kiss her again—and again and again—with restraint he was clearly having to work for.

Then he stopped altogether and just pulled her to him, wrapped his arms around her and held her with her cheek to his chest while her own arms somehow went around him, too.

"Yeah, no doubt about it—there has to be a wild streak hidden in you somewhere calling to me…" he murmured then, into her hair.

But there wasn't a wild streak in her, and Gia knew it. She just didn't tell him because it felt so fantastic to be held like that by him and she couldn't ruin that one moment with the truth.

Instead, she let herself have a few minutes in his arms, against him, before she gently unnestled herself from the cocoon and said, "I have to go…."

Like with the kiss, he didn't accept that instantly, tightening his grip for a moment before giving in. But when he gave in, Gia stood without hesitation because she knew if she didn't she was too likely to kiss him again.

Derek got to his feet, too, cupping one of those big hands of his around the back of her neck to walk her through the house.

"There won't be dirt on the menu, but what would you say to going to Sunday dinner at my grandmother's house with me tomorrow night?" he asked just as they reached his front door.

A big Camden family dinner.

Like a big Grant family dinner.

Where she'd be an outsider….

"I don't think that's a good idea," she said, her voice a bit gravelly from the kissing.

"My grandmother wants to talk to you about the Bronsons' health needs," he said. "And it just occurred to me that tomorrow would be the perfect time. She has connections with the best hospitals, the best doctors, the best care and management for geriatrics. But it's GiGi who has the inside line on all that stuff, not me, and you know the Bronsons' conditions, so it's really something that's better talked about without me as a go-between."

As much as Gia wanted to see him, she didn't want it to be at dinner with another big, close-knit family. She knew all too well what that was like and she wanted no part of it.

But she could hardly refuse when he put it in terms of helping Larry and Marion.

Still, she had to try....

"Couldn't we meet and talk about it some other time? It doesn't seem like a family dinner is—"

"There's always a ton of people around—not just family, never just family. And everybody mingles and talks—you and I and GiGi can just take a few minutes to chat as part of that, and then we can have a nice meal and I'll take you home.... Come on, you'll like GiGi— she's not too different from Marion—and you'll still have your whole Sunday before that free because hors d'oeuvres and drinks are at five, dinner is at six."

And she'd be with him again.

And she wanted to be.

And she knew she shouldn't want it or give in to it.

But she also wanted Larry and Marion to have the best care they could get.

Then, still standing at his front door, his hand still cupping her nape, he pulled her toward him as he leaned down and kissed her again.

As if *that* would help her decide!

And yet it did. Because when he stopped kissing her she said, "Okay. I guess…"

"Not enthusiastic, but I'll take it."

He kissed her again—the play of his tongue reminding her of their kisses on the patio—before he finally ended it and took his hand away.

"I'll pick you up a little before five. Comfortable, casual, but no jeans," he warned.

Gia nodded, trying to recover from the effects of that last kiss.

"Thanks for dinner," she said, remembering her manners belatedly as he walked her out to her car and she opened the driver's door, looking up at him again then.

His handsome face slid into a slow grin and he kissed her one more time before he said, "Drive safe."

"I will," she assured him, getting behind the wheel.

But that assurance was false, because as she put the key in the ignition and started the engine she realized that while she might have been careful about the wine, she hadn't realized that the kissing was even more heady, and she could only hope to focus enough to get herself home.

Where she didn't have a doubt that she'd relive the feel of him holding her, kissing her, right up until the minute she fell asleep.

Chapter Eight

"I can't believe I have to do this tonight," Gia said to Tyson on Sunday morning.

Tyson and Minna had broken up and he'd invited Gia upstairs for pancakes to tell her the news. The relationship had burned hot and fast, then fizzled, and he was taking it in stride. He'd just wanted Gia to know since she'd introduced them and there was the potential of her running into Minna at work. He'd also wanted her to be aware that there were no hard feelings on either his or Minna's part.

"It was just, you know, a good time," he'd concluded before asking what he'd missed while he was preoccupied. That was when Gia had told him that she'd agreed to go to the Camden Sunday dinner this evening with Derek.

"I'm kicking myself because I know it's bound to be just like the Grants' family dinners," she went on. "I'll walk in and get the squint-eye like I'm a geek who's wandered into cool-kid territory. Most of them won't bother to talk to me. The ones who do will be rude or nasty or will grill me like a captured spy. No matter what, I won't be good enough for them and I'll just want to be anywhere but there."

Tyson didn't refute any of that. Instead, he said, "At least you know going in that there's one thing different— you won't be *trying* to fit in or be accepted. You *are* an outsider with them. The Grants still treated you that way even after you'd been one of them for seven years."

"Still, I'm dreading it...." Except for the fact that she'd be with Derek, and she was worried about that for other reasons.

"Sharon went to a couple of the Camden Sunday dinners," Tyson told her. "She loved them—"

"I thought she complained about them."

"She did. But it was the fact that there *was* a mandatory Sunday dinner every week that she didn't like. She said the dinners themselves were good—fantastic food, booze, a big party. And you know Sharon—a lot of people means an audience, and she goes in like a lounge act and loves that. She just didn't like the Sunday after Sunday routine."

"Apparently she wasn't the only one of Derek's old girlfriends to use the Sunday dinners as a forum or to make a spectacle," Gia said, going on to tell him about the head shaving and the food policing.

"So it wasn't just nutcase Sharon and the two weirdos after her, this guy *does* go for—"

"He calls them unique, colorful or edgy." Gia supplied the terminology for her friend. "But your cousin and her friends were not his only venture into—"

"Wackjobs?"

"And bad girls who have led him astray," Gia added. But she decided suddenly that she wasn't going to tell Tyson about Derek's Las Vegas wedding and the subsequent disaster. Which was a little odd, because she'd always told Tyson everything and it made her feel slightly disloyal that she didn't.

But seeing how the event had affected Derek also made her feel protective of him and of what he'd confided in her, and that feeling won out.

Which only compounded what worried her in regards to Derek....

Tyson passed her the syrup as he said, "I'm betting that it won't be like the get-togethers with the Grants anyway. When you walked into any social situation involving Elliot's family, he forgot you were alive the minute he hit the door, but I don't think that's going to happen with this guy."

"Don't be too sure," Gia said, because it was actually what she expected.

"I don't know. Derek doesn't seem to want you out of his sight no matter where you are."

"What do you mean he doesn't want me out of his sight?" And why did the mere suggestion please her?

"He keeps an eye on you every minute—don't tell me you haven't noticed."

She hadn't. She'd thought she was the one always trying to catch glimpses of him. "I don't think so," she said, voicing her doubt again.

"Oh, yeah," Tyson insisted. "When we painted Larry and Marion's house, the minute he found out he wouldn't be working with you, he did some fast maneuvering to make sure he would. And every time you moved two steps away at the barbecue, he looked around till he spotted you again. The same at the yard sale. Plus, he hangs around after we're done doing whatever we're doing for Larry and Marion—he's always the last one to go. Unless I miss my guess, he's got it bad for you, G. He probably just wants you at this dinner so he can have you there himself."

"He said it was so I could talk to his grandmother about Larry and Marion's health care."

Tyson snickered. "I'm sure he did," he said knowingly.

"I'm not his type, Ty," she contended, even more convinced of that after hearing what Derek had said the night before.

"You're not a wackjob or a nutcase or completely loony tunes, no. And you're a long way from a bad girl," he added. "But there's a lot more to you and it's all great and unless I'm mistaken, ol' Derek Camden has taken notice."

"It doesn't matter," Gia claimed, emphasizing to herself that it *needed* not to matter.

"Yeah, he's probably still more like Elliot than *not* like Elliot," Tyson agreed.

"You don't like him…."

"Nah, I like him fine. But one-on-one I liked Elliot, too. I just didn't like him as your husband. He was lousy at it and his family treated you like dirt."

"Plus, Derek isn't the kind of guy who settles down with someone like me to have a normal life and a couple of normal kids. He goes for the thrill ride, and that's not me."

"Wow! Why do you sound so sad about that?"

"I don't!"

"Yes, you do! You were all perky when I said he keeps his eye on you, but that stuff about how wrong the two of you are for each other? It's like you just burst your own bubble."

Maybe she had.

But it was a bubble that needed to be burst.

"You *do* like him," Tyson said more carefully, repeating what he'd accused her of the very first time they'd talked about Derek. Only now it wasn't merely a question; there was some conviction in it.

"I do," she broke down and confessed. "Maybe I have a thing for bad boys."

"Maybe you do…" Tyson said ominously, under his breath.

"I know better, though," she swore. "I'm not going to let it go any further.…"

Tyson's eyebrows shot up. "How far have you let it go?"

Gia made a face. "You know…just some kissing.…" An understatement when the kissing was so fabulous that merely recalling it made her toes curl.

"God, be careful, G…" Tyson said with a voice full of concern.

"You're supposed to say, 'Sure you know better, Gia, and of course you won't let it go any further.'"

Tyson nodded, but he didn't say the lines she'd given him. Instead, he said, "Hey, I know how it is—you meet somebody and things click and even if you know better, that doesn't make them unclick. Just be careful," he repeated. "Maybe mess around with him, but don't get into more than that. A little fun, a little…release.… Just enough to boost your ego and remind you how you are much more than Elliot Grant deserved. But other than that—"

"I know."

"Can you do just that?" Tyson asked as if he didn't think she could.

She shrugged. "You can," she said as if that meant she could, too.

"Yeah, I just did with Minna. She just did with me. But you… I don't know, G…. You haven't had anybody since Elliot. It could be a rebound thing—and I don't want to see you just close your eyes and fall…."

"My eyes are open," she said.

"And how clearly are they seeing?"

"Clearly enough to see that Derek has close ties with a big family that's done really lousy things to other people. Clearly enough to see that Derek could very well be like Elliot and be more surface than substance. Clearly enough to see that he's been through a lot of women and the only ones who keep his interest for any amount of time are nothing like me. Clearly enough to see that I'm a babe in the woods when it comes to dating again and am not ready to do anything serious."

Just not clearly enough to see her way past how terrific looking Derek was. Or how sexy. Or how good it felt to be with him. Or how wonderful it was to have him hold her and kiss her. Or how much she just wanted to be with him again the minute they were apart….

And even though she didn't say all that, she knew that Tyson could tell, because his expression was concerned and helpless.

"Just be careful," he said a third time. "Just get in, hook up, get out—can you do that to get it out of your system?"

Gia laughed, thinking about how much more than kissing she'd wanted the night before.

"Maybe," she said. "I can tell you that it isn't white dresses and wedding chapels and picket fences and bouncing babies that are on my mind when I'm with him, that's for sure."

"Oh, geez, you do want him," Tyson said somewhat forlornly. "Then go for it, I guess. But if you start picturing white dresses and wedding chapels and picket fences and bouncing babies, run for the hills!"

"I promise."

For Gia, the Camden family Sunday dinner was a combination of good and bad.

Derek *did* stay by her side through the entire thing. That was a vast improvement over how Elliot had treated her at similar gatherings.

But merely being faced with the big, obviously close-knit family was intimidating to her.

She gave the Camdens credit for going out of their way to be friendly and welcoming, because they were. Unfailingly. But there were so many of them. And after being introduced, after chatting warmly, when talk would turn even for brief moments to things between Derek and other members of his family that she couldn't participate in, Gia flashed back to Grant family gatherings in which she'd been excluded and felt invisible.

She also gave the Camdens credit, because not a single pocket of conversation had stopped when she came within hearing range. There weren't any withering, disapproving looks cast her way. There was no indication that there was anything secretive going on.

But Gia was still very aware of the fact that she was not a part of things when the family fussed over the pregnant Jani, or everyone teased the newly married matriarch, Georgianna, or focused on the antics of Lang's three-year-old son, Carter, or bantered about when weddings should be held for the engaged couples among them.

So while the whole affair lacked the ugly overtones

that had come with the Grants, still—despite every effort by Derek and the rest of his family to put her at ease—Gia just couldn't relax or enjoy herself. And she was never as relieved as when it was finally over with and she and Derek were walking to his car.

"Okay, now breathe…" he joked, sounding like a birthing coach.

"Haven't I been?"

"*Have* you been?" he challenged. "I don't think I've ever had anybody at Sunday dinner who was more tense. The whole time. And I haven't seen you like that before. Are we that scary?"

They hadn't been scary at all. It was just her. And her own baggage. So she said, "No. Did I seem scared?"

He opened the passenger door of his sports car for her to get in, frowning rather than answering her.

Once he went around and got behind the wheel, Gia veered from the topic by saying, "It was really nice of your grandmother to offer to get Larry and Marion in to her primary-care physician even though he isn't ordinarily accepting new patients. I'd like it if they saw someone new. The doctor they've been using acts like she doesn't want to be bothered with them."

"Will they switch doctors? Especially to a doctor a Camden arranges for them?"

"I think they'll be glad for better care no matter how it comes about."

"Good. I'm glad."

"And the food was great!" she continued, trying to distract him when he looked at her out of the corner of his eye and she knew he was still thinking about how uncomfortable she'd been. "You're grandmother's homemade biscuits were better than any I've ever had."

"She loves it when anyone likes her cooking—"

"It was nice of her to send some home. I was kind of surprised that she cooks, though."

"She does everything. Farm girl, remember?"

"I just wouldn't think that someone in her position would—"

"Her position?" he repeated with some humor in his tone. "That would make her laugh—she'd be the first one to say that she isn't the queen of England."

When they pulled into her driveway, Gia was relieved that she'd effectively filled the short drive to her house with small talk.

Derek stopped the engine and got out, and so did Gia, not waiting for him to come around to her side.

As they went up to her house, he nodded toward her porch swing. Her porch formed an L around the front and one side of her house, and the swing hung from chains hooked into the porch's roof. It faced the street at the rear-most portion of the L, between the side of her house and the Bronsons' garage. It was so far back from street lights and in such deep shadow without her porch light on that it was almost completely hidden in darkness. But he'd been there when it wasn't dark and seen it.

"It's a nice night and it's early yet," he said. "How about we sit out here for a little while? Or did you have something you needed to get done tonight for work tomorrow?"

"No, nothing. That sounds good," she said, realizing only in that moment that she hadn't thought beyond the dinner and so hadn't considered whether or not to ask him in. Had he not made the suggestion she might have been at risk of having him say good-night at the door and leave.

And she wouldn't have liked that.

"Can I make coffee or pour some iced tea? Or I have

soda," she offered, beginning to come back to herself now that she was on home turf.

"No, thanks. Just go in and put your biscuits away. I'll wait out here for you."

"I'll be right back," she answered as she unlocked and opened her front door.

Inside, out of his sight, she finally did take a few of those deep breaths he'd recommended.

Then she popped into her guest bathroom for a quick check in the mirror. No mascara smudges. Blush still adding color to her cheekbones. Left to fall loose, her crazy curly hair was still as tamed as it ever got. And the khaki slacks, white tank top and tailored red shirt she wore open all remained wrinkle-free.

The only thing she did was reapply a little lip gloss, and then she went back outside.

She still didn't turn on the porch light because it attracted bugs. In the dark, the swing was in such deep shadow that had she not known Derek was there she wouldn't have noticed him.

But he was there. Sitting in the center of the swing, angled to his left, with an ankle propped on the opposite knee and his arm across the top slat, waiting for her.

Once her eyes had adjusted and she could see him, she was struck all over again by how ruggedly handsome he was. And after not having any time alone with him through the dinner, it felt as if this was only the beginning of her time with him today.

He'd left her no option but to sit in the lee of his arm and that was just what she did.

When she was fully settled, he said, "Now tell me why the hell you were so stressed out tonight. Did I do something?"

"No," she assured him without hesitation. "I really appreciated that you never left my side. It was just me...."

"It can't be that you don't like crowds—there weren't any more people there tonight than at your barbecue and you were just fine. Was it us? All of us? Too many of us? Was somebody there an old lover?" he added with some levity.

Gia managed to laugh. "No, it was just me.... My ex-husband came from a family like yours...sort of...."

"A family like mine? In what way?"

"Big. Close. In business together," she said, sanitizing it. "I was married to Elliot Grant—of Grant Moving and Storage."

"I know the company. We used them when we moved our offices from three different buildings into the one we're in now. They do commercial moving and storage, not residential, right? They move businesses, corporations, things like that."

"Right. I'm not surprised you've used them, they make sure to keep their competition to a minimum, especially in Colorado."

"I guess I didn't know it was owned by one big family the way Camden Superstores is."

"Uh-huh. Elliot is one of eight kids and he has thirteen cousins who all—along with his parents, aunts and uncles—own and operate the company."

"Those numbers beat ours—they *are* a big family."

"Uh-huh."

"Okay, come on, stop holding out on me. I told you last night about the worst mess I've made. So what gives with the ex and the ex's family that triggered you looking like you wanted to hide under a table all night tonight?"

She'd already learned that Derek was insightful and perceptive and observant, that there wasn't much he missed. It was part of what she liked about him. Except maybe now.

"Grant family dinners were not fun," she said, knowing he wouldn't be satisfied until she was honest with him.

"Were they bigger than tonight's?"

"No, about the same—some of the cousins and one brother live out of state, where they keep an iron-fisted presence in a couple of other places. But the Grants weren't very welcoming to people who married into the family—"

She was close enough to Derek to see his confused expression. "They weren't?"

"Oh, no. *Grants are born Grants or they aren't really Grants,*" she said, adopting the imperious tone that they had used. "Elliot's mother and the other wives of the older generation aren't even considered *real* Grants. Long marriages have given them more insider status and made them as bad as the real Grants when it comes to those of us who were new. But their sisters-in-law—the two women born into that generation of Grants—never let them forget that they weren't *real* Grants and if they got divorced, that would be it for them."

"That would be *it* for them…." he repeated melodramatically and with a slight chuckle. "Now, *that* sounds scary. Would they be hunted down? Shot like dogs? What?"

"No, but…" Gia shrugged. "Anyone who isn't a Grant is an outsider. Divorce makes you not only an outsider but an enemy. And outsiders are treated bad enough. Enemies… Well, I think that can actually get dangerous…."

He frowned again. "Okay, explain—dangerous how, and you only *think* that, you don't know for sure?"

"I didn't know a lot about the Grants *for sure.* I wasn't

privy to inside information, and when it came to the business, Elliot would say that it was nothing I needed to know—"

"Ooh, that sounds familiar," Derek admitted. "That's what my great-grandfather used to say."

"But I was married to Elliot for seven years and there were things I overheard here and there. Sometimes I'd pieced it together with what I heard elsewhere…."

"Like what?"

"Like something I'd hear on the news later about vandalism to another moving company's trucks or a competitor's storage facility catching fire. Once I heard something about being underbid, then later they were all laughing about how that guy's rubber wouldn't ever be hitting the road again…." She shrugged once more. "You kind of get an idea for what happened. And then I saw what went on when a sister-in-law divorced one of Elliot's brothers—"

"They weren't just thugs in business?"

"I don't know that the Grants are thugs," she said. "I know that they pay to have anything done that they don't want to do themselves, and I can't see any of them actually getting their hands dirty—"

"So you figure they hire out the dirty work."

"I only know that they aren't upstanding people. They have power and money and feel entitled to do whatever they want—or as they see it, *need*—to make money and succeed and get their way. They aren't ethical—they make sure they're friends with and big contributors to other people in power, and that's helped them buy their way out of anything."

"Why does it feel like somewhere in your head you said *like the Camdens?*"

So he *was* a mind reader….

But when she didn't confirm or deny it, he didn't push it. "What went on when your sister-in-law wanted out?" he asked instead.

"She was welcome to go. Empty-handed and without her little boy."

"Who had Grant blood so he *was* a real Grant."

"That's how it works. And like I said, they have lots of money and power and really good lawyers and friends who are judges. First they did a horrible smear campaign against Linda that made her look like the most unfit parent on the planet—which she wasn't at all! But by the time they were finished, the best she got was three hours of visitation every other weekend, under court-ordered supervision by the Grants. Then they made even those three hours impossible for her to actually ever arrange and no matter how hard she tried, there just wasn't anything she could do. By the time I left Elliot, Linda had only seen Bobby twice in six months."

"For three hours, with an in-law watching."

"I felt awful for her. She just lost that little boy to them and there was nothing she could do."

"And you couldn't risk backing her up?"

"I offered…behind Elliot's back," she said in a quieter voice, knowing it wasn't rational but still somewhat leery of bringing down any of the Grants' wrath. "But her lawyer said it wouldn't help. It was just my word against what looked like proof that she was unfit, and that anything I said would just get shot down. I was still willing, but Linda said no. She said she didn't want to be responsible for what my life would be like with the Grants—or even with Elliot—if I did."

Derek took a deep breath and exhaled. "Why did you marry this guy—and into all of this?"

"I honestly, honestly have no idea. He seemed like the

nicest guy. He's very personable—you can ask Tyson. Even he liked Elliot until I was years into the marriage. Elliot is smart. Good-looking. Charming... I knew he was close to his family, that they all worked for the family business and that it was very successful, but I had no idea of anything beyond that. And to tell you the truth, I had fantasies of belonging to a big, close family—"

"You'd only had your grandparents and you'd lost them just before," he recalled.

"Right. Plus, while we were dating I only met his parents and a few of his brothers and sisters—I never went to a big family dinner or saw the dynamics of it all. His family was kind of standoffish, but Elliot wasn't. As I told Tyson at the time that I was going out with Elliot, not his family...."

"But when you got engaged...still no inkling?"

"No. They warmed up a little and I thought that was just the beginning, that it would get better from there. They threw a big wedding shower for us, but at that point Elliot was all about being with me and we were the guests of honor, so everything was revolving around us—like with the wedding, too. It was only afterward that I started to see the way things really were...."

"With his family. But what about him? Did the marriage go instantly south, too, or did you keep on the blinders awhile longer?"

The blinders...

He was referring to what she'd said the night they'd walked home after having ice cream.

"No, the marriage didn't *immediately* go south," she said, finding it more difficult to talk about this than about the entire Grant family. "For the first year or so we were like any married couple—happy, settling in, getting to know each other, in love—"

"How long did you date before you got married?"

"We met at a benefit for the Botanical Gardens and there was six months of dating, another six engaged and planning the wedding."

"And after the first year of marriage?"

"It was a case of a relationship going bad by inches," she said, again with some difficulty. "The marriage suffered at the expense of how close he was to his family. They came first—and I mean that literally. A phone call from any one of them and he went running day or night for even the smallest things. It didn't matter if I was miserably sick, if I needed him for something, if we were on a vacation—everything stopped, he went to his family and I was just out of luck. Little by little it wore on me."

"But you were *his* family—*you* should have come before anything except maybe an emergency somewhere else," Derek said, as if what she was describing was unfathomable to him.

"That's how I thought it should be, but that's not how it was. Once, about five years in, I was in the emergency room with a broken wrist and his brother got a flat tire—"

"And he left a wife with a broken bone to fix a flat?"

"He did. And he didn't come back. I had to call Tyson to pick me up when my wrist was set. I was really getting the picture by then that I would never be even a close second to his family."

"Is that when you left him?"

"No. I was having doubts about him, about us, about the future—"

"About the fact that the kissing had stopped?"

Oh, more of her words haunting her—from when she'd marveled that Larry and Marion still kissed without either of them having to force it....

But she was in this far, she decided she might as well not try to sugarcoat anything.

"Yeah, the kissing had stopped. By then I was like…" This just wasn't easy—not to talk about and relive, and not to explain. "When Elliot and I first met, I was something he really wanted—the way a kid wants a Christmas present. So he was great. He couldn't have shown more interest, he couldn't see enough of me, he wanted to please me any way he could. He swept me off my feet—"

"Then it wasn't Christmas morning anymore."

"At first it was still good, except for his family, but I just thought…you know, *in-laws*…" she said with exasperation. "I blamed them for calling him away all the time, not him for running to them, and I hadn't started to get an idea of their other…practices…so I just thought they were a pain in the neck."

"Then the newness of the favorite Christmas toy wore off?"

Gia shrugged. "Yes," she said because there was no better way to describe it. "He barely knew I was alive or cared if I was," she admitted. "*Whatever*—that got to be a word I hated! Everything I tried to talk to him about, everything I asked of him, he wouldn't so much as look away from watching TV or playing a video game or texting or doing something else on his phone, and he'd just say, 'Whatever.' Which meant that he hadn't heard a word that I'd said. It just got to be like I didn't exist. Or if I did, it was only on the very edges of his life. I guess I was the Christmas gift on display on a shelf in the living room rather than a totally forgotten one hidden on a shelf in a closet. But I was still just stuck on a shelf."

"And you stayed for seven years?"

"We were married," she said, "and I kept hoping

that things would change, that the spark would come back...."

The spark she'd tried putting back only to be rejected....

"What made you finally leave—especially given that these people were not kind to anybody who did?"

"I'd been thinking about it for a while when Elliot decided we should start having kids—which was just after what I'd watched happen to Linda."

"So faced with a token marriage to a husband who neglected you and pressure to have kids you would lose to the clan if you ever left after that—"

"And the fact that by then I had some idea of the Grants' seedy side and I was not proud to be part of it even by association—"

"You decided to get out."

"I did. Which became a nightmare of a battle for both me and for Tyson—he was my lawyer against the Grants' *team* of lawyers through a process that they dragged out for three years."

"Even without kids and a custody fight?"

"I'd inherited my grandparents' place when they died, and Elliot said he knew more about those kinds of things than I did, so he should take care of it. He decided the best thing to do was to sell it. But I never saw any of the money from it—he said it was safe and sound for the future—"

"But without a future with him, that money was rightfully yours."

"It was. And Tyson went after it—"

"Which set off a three-year battle?"

"We fought over that for two and a half of the three years. That was when Tyson and I finally gave up the idea of seeing any of that money. Instead, Elliot offered me this place—only because his last tenants had been college kids and it was completely trashed. But by then, I just wanted it all over with, so I agreed."

"And that was when you met the Bronsons...."

"When I got the house, yes."

"How long have you actually been divorced?"

"A year."

"And since then? Have this guy and his family left you alone? Or are we at risk of a drive-by shooting sitting out here like this?"

"It's pretty dark back in this corner, so I think we're safe," she joked. "No, once it was over, I stopped existing for the Grants. I saw my former mother-in-law with one of Elliot's sisters and two of his brothers at a restaurant not long ago and they all looked right through me, as if we'd never met."

"I'm sorry," Derek said sympathetically.

"It's no big deal."

"Not only for you getting snubbed by your former in-laws, but for all of it."

Gia laughed. "Well, that's more than Elliot ever said."

Derek bent the elbow of the arm resting on the slat behind her so he could bring one hand forward and move her hair from the front of her shoulder to the back of it. Once he had, his fingers returned again to brush a few strokes against the side of her neck as he peered into her face, studying her. His feather-light touch eased her tension and replaced it with something tingly and titillating that scattered through her like glitter.

After a few minutes of studying her as if he was searching for something, he shook his head and said, "How that guy could watch TV or text or play video games rather than look at you, talk to you, *kiss* you... I'm finding it hard to understand."

"You? The king of losing interest?" she teased.

"Me. Yeah…"

Just saying the word *kiss* had triggered the need in Gia, so when he leaned forward then to do just that, she met him halfway.

And while it hadn't been on her mind for more than a few seconds in advance, the first meeting of mouths really was what she needed in so many ways. Not only had she been longing to have him kiss her again since she'd stopped him the night before, but it helped her to believe that she hadn't completely lost her appeal—the way just recalling the end of her marriage had made her feel.

Gia was instantly lost in kissing him. Her hand went to his chest without his encouragement this time, and when his other arm came around to enclose her in that splendid circle of biceps, she sank into him.

Lips parted and tongues reconvened with giddiness at the reunion, and everything else faded into oblivion— the hours that had passed without him, the family dinner, even her own past. There was just Derek and kissing him and being held against him again in those arms.

But her hand was like a brick wall between them, and she didn't want that.

So she snaked it around his shoulder, moving her other arm, too, so she could have both hands pressed to his strong back. And her front to his….

She hadn't realized how much her body had been craving that until she got there—to have her own arms around him, to absorb the feel of his back through her palms, to have her breasts in contact with his well-muscled chest.

She felt her nipples turn into tiny pebbles and wondered if he could feel it, too, since the tank top's built-in bra wasn't much of a barrier.

And yet, at the same time, it was enough to blunt sensations that she suddenly didn't want blunted....

Oh, that was a dangerous thought!

But it was true. Her body was craving things she'd made it stop craving a long time ago. Things she'd stopped thinking about so she wouldn't miss them. Things she'd thought might seem strange to do again with someone else.

Only that wasn't the case. Not with Derek. Instead, wanting him, wanting his hands on her, came naturally and it was all she could think about.

She deepened their kiss as a new drive came to life in her. And she upped the sexiness quotient of their tongues at play, entreating and tempting him as she expanded her chest into his and kneaded the taut muscles of his back through the sport shirt he was wearing with slacks that fit him so well that during his grandmother's dinner she'd stolen every opportunity to catch a glimpse of his great rear end in them.

Merely recalling that caused her to draw one hand down and forward to his thigh, wanting also to know if it was as thick and hard as those slacks seemed to hint at. And when she found that it was, her nipples got tighter still, nearly aching for his hand on them.

She sometimes liked to sit on her porch swing in the dark and just look out unseen at passing cars or neighbors walking by, but never had she been as grateful for those deep shadows as she was when Derek intensified the kiss himself and one of his hands trailed down to the hem of her outer shirt and then from there under her tank top.

Something that was more than a sigh but less than a moan rumbled in her throat at that first moment of his big, warm hand meeting skin.

The feel of a man's touch...

It had been a long time.

But more than that, this was the feel of Derek's touch, and there was something electrifying in that contact not only of skin on skin, but of his skin on hers.

She didn't know if he knew how much she needed more of that contact or if he needed it, too, but after only a moment of resting his hand on her bare back he brought it around to her front and upward.

Her breath caught when he enclosed her breast in his grasp. When his fingers pressed into her flesh and her nipple turned harder still, nestling into the center of his palm.

Gentle then less gentle, firm then less firm—he caressed and kneaded and pulled and pushed her just so, just right, just enough to arouse and inspire her to thoughts of more. More of him. More of his touch. More of his mouth on more parts of her....

She wanted that.

She wanted every bit of it. Every bit of him. She wanted to know every inch of him with her own hands, her own mouth, and she wanted him to know every inch of her.

I could take him inside....

Her breast swelled even more boldly into his hand with that thought, and her own hand went up a few inches on his thigh.

But only a few.

Just short of reaching that part of him that she really wanted to touch.

But despite her talk with Tyson that morning, despite how much she wanted Derek—and she wanted him so much she was almost ashamed of herself—she just wasn't sure.

Could she merely mess around with this man, have

only a little fun—enough to boost her own ego—and then go on about her business without a blip?

It wasn't something she'd ever done before. And she just wasn't sure if she could now....

Be careful— Tyson had said it three times and the warning pinballed through her mind, rejected by pangs of desire only to warn her again, be rejected again, then warn her once more.

Once more was enough.

Damn it all anyway....

She groaned softly, covered Derek's hand at her breast to press him tightly to her as if that would help engrave the feeling into her skin forever, and then she let go of his hand and ended the kiss by increments.

"I don't know if we should be doing this...." she said. "I don't know if *I* should be doing this...."

His fingers pushed into her flesh once more as if he was doing the same thing she had—memorizing the sensation to take with him—before he let go of her and took his hand out from under her shirt.

He didn't say anything as he dropped his forehead to the top of hers, stayed there a moment, then kissed her again—so sweetly she had second thoughts about why anything she did with him could be anything other than right.

But she couldn't let herself get carried away, and when that kiss ended, too, she bit back the words that would have invited him inside after all.

She heard him exhale and knew that he was working at regaining some control before he said, "Work tomorrow... Monday," as if trying to put order to things. "You're meeting with bankers for the Bronsons...."

"I am."

He nodded. "Okay. I'll call you after. You can tell me what happened."

But what about this? What about us?

That was what went through her mind before she told herself there wasn't any *us* and *this* probably shouldn't be anything, either.

And just the fact that she'd had these thoughts warned her that she might not be able to take anything she did with him as lightly as she needed to, so she was right not to go any further.

He stood then, keeping hold of her hand to bring her to her feet, too, and walked her to her door.

"Oh, what you do to me..." he said when they got there and his glance went through the screen, as if he'd also been thinking about taking things inside.

Gia wasn't sure whether to apologize for not asking him in, so she didn't say anything but "Drive home safe."

"Always," he said, pulling her toward him again by the hand he was still holding. He wrapped his other arm around her and kissed her once more so thoroughly, so intensely, so temptingly, that she melted all over again and very nearly threw reason out and dragged him inside anyway.

But then that kiss ended and he smiled down at her and said, "Night, Gia."

There was enough finality to that for her to find some acceptance, too, and she said, "Good night."

But when he kissed her yet again, when the tip of his tongue teased hers, when his hand just barely brushed her breast before he said another ragged-voiced goodnight and left her to watch him go down her porch steps to his car, she wasn't sure she'd made the right choice.

Because her body was screaming at her for it.

And the pure and simple truth was that she was sorry she'd sent him away....

Chapter Nine

"Tonight. Dressed up—heels, hose, hair, the whole works. I'll be at your house at seven. I have some things to tell you that have to do with the Bronsons and then something else to tell you, too. Then I'll take you out to the best dinner money can buy—even though you've earned much more than that for what you've done for your neighbors and for a whole lot of other people."

That was what Derek had said to Gia when he'd called her at work on Tuesday morning.

Mysterious, intriguing, a little flattering.

How could she say no?

Especially when she wanted to see him so badly she might have gone running if he'd just snapped his fingers.

Plus, she had a dress....

So she left work early Tuesday afternoon and went home to shower and shampoo and condition her hair.

As it was drying she scrunched it to actually add more curl so it was even fuller, with extra flair for fanciness.

Tonight's makeup routine included eye shadow and liner, as well as a bit more blush and a second layer of mascara.

After that, she put on her thigh-high black nylons with her matching lace bikinis and strapless bra. Then the dress.

Slinky and black, it fit like a second skin. It had an off-the-shoulder neckline that went straight across, and didn't miss a curve all the way to a few inches above her knees.

She'd loved the dress when she'd bought it four years ago but she'd never had the chance to wear it, and was glad to find that she still could.

Since Derek was so tall, the height of her heels didn't matter, so she went with the strappy black four-inch sandals.

She was just applying a pale mauve lipstick rather than simple lip gloss when her doorbell rang at seven sharp.

"Wowza!" Derek said, his expression reflecting how much he liked what he saw when she opened the door.

Right back at you, Gia thought as she thanked him.

She'd seen him in work suits and had no idea what made this suit different. But was it ever! He could have been inaugurated president in it.

It was midnight blue with a grayish cast and it accentuated to perfection his broad shoulders and divinely shaped torso. Under it he wore a dove-gray shirt with a matching tie, and she'd never seen anyone outside of a fashion magazine look as dynamic as he did.

"You clean up pretty well yourself," she said as she let him in, fighting not to close her eyes and just breath in the clean woodsy scent of his cologne when he stepped in front of her.

Then she closed the door and turned to find him ogling her from the center of her living room.

"I wanted you dressed up, but you've blown me away, lady," he said. "Look at you... Positively sultry."

Me, sultry?

But the way he was looking at her confirmed that he liked what he saw as his gaze went from top to bottom to top again. With those gorgeous blue eyes wide.

"Turn and give me the whole thing."

"No," she demurred, beginning to feel self-conscious. Pleased, but self-conscious.

But he was determined because when she got farther into the room to join him he walked around her, making a full circle.

"Wowza from all angles" was his conclusion. "And here I am, just wanting to take it apart...." he mused under his breath before he surprised her by catching her hand in his to pull her to him so he could kiss her.

Wowza...

Then, just when he'd kissed her so thoroughly her knees were weak, he let go of her, and it took Gia a minute to regroup.

When she had, she found him smiling at her as he seemed to start over. "Hi."

Gia laughed at him. "Hi," she parroted.

"How was your day?" he asked mundanely.

"Good. How was yours?"

"Productive. I bought the Bronsons' house."

Screeching halt.

Gia froze and she could actually feel the color drain from her face. "You bought the Bronsons' house?"

"I did."

"Out from under them?" she said, her voice louder as panic began to hit. "Why would you do that? That's just what they were afraid of from you! Do you hate those poor people or what? What did they ever do to the Camdens? You're no better than the ones who ran them out of their hotel—"

"Whoa! Whoa! Whoa! After the time we've spent together, that's still where you go? Come on—"

"You bought their house out from under them!" she repeated, louder still.

"Think about that, Gia.... How would I do that?"

"They're behind in their payments. The bank has threatened foreclosure. You're the *Camdens*—you could own the bank for all I know. You have more money than God and probably more power. You strolled in and got the bank to sell it to you right out from under Larry and Marion!"

He shook his head. "Take a breath."

She couldn't. Her mind was racing. Her heart was pounding. Even her breathing felt restricted.

Derek took her by the shoulders—bare shoulders that responded to the feel of his hands on them even as she was whirling with shock—and guided her to the sofa. "Sit down and hear me out," he commanded.

Her knees were weak all over again so she did sit, terrified that she'd pushed Larry and Marion right into the lion's den when they'd warned her not to let the Camdens be involved.

Once she was sitting, she kept her eyes on Derek. Only now it wasn't because he looked fantastic, it was because she was right back to wondering if she had to.

He sat down beside her, angled toward her, his brow furrowed. "Think a little better of me, would you?"

"First the Camdens who came before you ran the

Bronsons out of their hotel and now you've taken their house! What do you want me to think?"

His lips went tight and thin before he seemed to give in to something. Then he said, "I'm trusting you by saying this...."

He paused, obviously still weighing whether or not to say it.

Then he said, "The Bronsons got a raw deal at the hands of H.J. and my grandfather—"

An admission of guilt.

The Grants would never—ever—have made one.

But rather than that seeming like a good thing, all Gia could think was that she might have to use it in court, testifying that he'd said it in order to try to fix this for her neighbors.

"But I...my family now...had nothing to do with that," he went on. "And not one of us would ever do something like that to anyone. Or stand for it being done in our name. No one is more sorry than I am that it was ever done. So what we're trying to do now is make it up to them. I did *not* buy their house out from under them! What I did was pay off their loan. The title is free and clear *in their name*—that's the first thing I wanted to talk to you about," he said. "You told me yesterday what happened at the bank—"

The bank would agree to refinance only if there was a co-signer, and even if Gia did that, the payments were still higher than the Bronsons could comfortably afford. Gia knew it was better for them to sell and move into her basement. But she couldn't make that decision for them, so she'd left it up to them to think about and decide. Then Derek had called and she'd told him.

"I know you'd be fine having them move in here," he was saying. "But I also know—because you told me—

that they'd rather stay in their house. So I made it so they can. They own it free and clear—*they* own it, not me, not any Camden. The title will come to them, in the name of Larry and Marion Bronson, without another soul attached to it. If they wanted, they could sell it next week and come away with every penny of the money in *their* pockets, and if they haven't done that when both of them pass away, it's theirs to leave to whomever they choose."

Gia studied him, searching for a sign that he wasn't telling the truth, mentally scanning for a hole in what he was telling her. But she didn't find any sign, any hole, and she calmed down. But only slightly.

"There's also an account opened for them," Derek continued. "I'll make sure it's funded to pay the taxes and insurance, any upkeep and utilities—everything that has to do with the house for as long as it's theirs. The account is in their names and yours so you can access it for them. It only needs you and them to sign the signature cards and it's ready to go. And again, we'll deposit into it but we have no access once the money is there—like the donation account you set up for them before. No access to the money and no claim on the house *whatsoever*—not now, not later, *never*."

"That's very generous.…" she said. But only tentatively, because he'd raised all her red flags again and it wasn't easy for her to lower them.

"I'm not finished," he said patiently. "We want to pay for someone to come in and help with the cleaning and look after whatever they might need—it can be live-in, round-the-clock care or whatever they'll be comfortable with. And as their needs change, so can the help that comes in—I'll leave it to you to talk to them about what they want now and we'll reassess whenever things change."

"Okay…" she said quietly, still afraid this was all too good to be true.

"I know they're just barely warming up to me, but I want to build on that so I can keep in contact to make whatever alterations need to be made as time goes by. GiGi called her doctor and told him that any bills not covered by the Bronsons' insurance are to be sent to us—that includes anything they need healthwise, now or later."

Gia nodded and she knew that it was her eyes that were wide now because all he was explaining stunned her.

He smiled slightly. "Relax, will you? I came in to assess how much damage was done by them losing their hotel years ago. I watched and listened so I could learn what they need, and I waited to see what you could accomplish for them. But now that I have the whole picture, I can see that the damage was extensive and the needs are far reaching, and even your best efforts aren't going to save them. So let me. We owe them that."

Another admission of guilt.

"We're going to make sure that they have *anything* they need from here on out," he assured. "We're going to make sure they're comfortable, that they're well taken care of and that for what's left of their lives, they're unburdened. But if they're still opposed to accepting it all from us, until I can build on the crack I've made in the ice, I'm going to count on you to keep running interference. And I'm definitely going to count on you to let us know if something happens suddenly that changes their needs or calls for more help—"

"And what's in it for you?" she heard herself ask, thinking about her ex-husband and his family again, concern overcoming her.

"Nothing. This is straight restitution, nothing else. If you think it's better for them not to even know it's all coming from us, even that's okay. If it will make them happier, you can say the house was paid off by an anonymous donor. Or I even have something else you can tell them—it won't be true, but it might make them feel better. That's the second part...."

"There's more?" she said, unsure how there could be.

"You and the Bronsons opened our eyes to the needs of the elderly in general, so the Camden Foundation is developing a program to provide this type of assistance to whoever needs it. What we do for the Bronsons is separate, but I'm assuming that they have friends and know other people in their own age bracket who can benefit from this kind of program, and if you think they'd feel better believing that what's coming to them is no more than any of their friends can access, let them think that."

"Seems like what you're talking about for them is more than anyone is going to get through a foundation, so they'd see through that. Plus, I think they'd like to know that you're admitting what was done to them was wrong—"

She could tell that was a sticky subject by the arch of his eyebrows and the resignation in his expression. "We don't need any credit, but we don't need the negative attention stirred up either, if that could be kept to a minimum."

Gia could understand that they were trying to live down a reputation that this generation might not deserve and that bringing up old wrongs wouldn't help. But she couldn't vouch for what Larry and Marion might do, so she could only say, "I'll do what I can."

Then, as more of what he'd told her sank in, she said, "So you set up a program that can help any elderly people who need it, and you did that with just the wave of a wand?"

He shrugged and she saw humility in the acknowledgment that yes, he had that ability. But what he said was, "The criteria are being hashed out now and put in place. By the first of the month, people can apply for help and if they qualify, it'll be there for them."

"For just any older people in need? No one in particular who might have some history with you the way Larry and Marion do?"

"For any elderly people in need. Before this, we just weren't really seeing that there *is* a need. But my grandmother is seventy-five—I told you, the thought of her being in the position the Bronsons are in…" He shook his head a second time. "We wouldn't want that. The Bronsons' situation got us all thinking, so we wanted to do what we can to help. I know what you think of us, but we really are trying to do better than what was done before…."

Gia was still looking for an ulterior motive. The Grants would have had one, because they weren't about actually doing good, they were just about cover-ups to make themselves *look* good.

But there just didn't seem to be an ulterior motive here. Derek had even admitted that he and his family bore some guilt. He'd been open with her, honest. And the scope of what he was giving to the Bronsons, what he was going to provide for other people, was impressive.

She thought that she might just have to concede that the Camdens—at least the current Camdens—were different than the Grants. That they acted with ethics and integrity, that they genuinely wanted to atone for whatever was done before them and give back. That they really were a different ilk than her former in-laws.

"This is all for real? You're serious," she said then, the shadow of disbelief hovering.

"About it all," he confirmed. "But you don't have to believe me—tomorrow you can confirm with the bank and see for yourself."

The fact that he wasn't going to any other lengths to prove himself, that he was willing to have his actions speak louder than his words was what put it over the top for her and she finally believed him.

"I don't think just saying thanks is enough...." she muttered as it began to genuinely register with her.

Derek put his hand on her knee then, and she instantly flashed back to having that hand on her breasts Sunday night. And to how much she'd wanted that again ever since.

But this time his touch wasn't sexual—except in what it roused in her. It was comforting and imploring at the same time as he looked into her eyes and said, "I was also serious about how amazingly beautiful you are if you'd just stop looking at me like I pulled the rug out from under you."

"I was afraid you had," she said. "Out from under me and the Bronsons."

"Nope. But I also don't want to minimize your part in all of this—you did so much for your neighbors and you're really responsible for showing us the overall problems. So we thought we might like to call the fund the Gia Grant Fund...."

Oh.

"The Gia Grant Fund..." she repeated.

"Within the Camden Foundation. Would that be okay?"

"I don't know.... It seems so weird to have something named after me. This wasn't that big of a deal—I was just trying to help Larry and Marion. Shouldn't I be dead or something before my name gets put on anything?"

"No!" he said with a laugh. "It's just recognition for what you've done. And we'd also like to invite you to be on the committee that will go through the applications so you'll have a vote on who gets what. It doesn't pay anything, though—to us or to anyone else who sits on our committees. We want all the money within the foundation to go toward the causes we support, so we run it, and we recruit and badger people to help out."

"I'd...be willing to do that...." Gia said, suddenly finding herself a little misty at the thought of it all. And very impressed with this man. And with his family.

It was a turnaround for her, and Gia looked at Derek through new eyes.

Not that he looked any better to her than he had, because that wasn't possible—he was just as drop-dead gorgeous as she'd registered the very first time she'd seen him. But she suddenly saw more substance to him than she'd given him credit for before, and that just made him all the more appealing.

"Dinner..." she said then, realizing that she needed something to get her to her feet and out of there. Because admiring him, appreciating him in new ways, only compounded feelings that had been set in motion Sunday night. And all she really wanted to do at that moment was what he'd said he wanted to do to her earlier—take his clothes off.

"Dinner..." he echoed, though in a quiet tone that lacked conviction while his eyes held hers and he began to massage her knee, sending little shards of light from that spot all through her. "Are you starving?" he asked then.

She was.

But for him....

That thought caused her to laugh a little, to smile at him, all of it infused with unintentional innuendo that he read because he mirrored that smile and a knowing look came into his blue eyes.

"The reservation isn't for a while...." he informed her, a question in his statement.

"No?" she answered buoyantly.

"But you said no the other night...." he reminded her, making it clear they *were* on the same wavelength.

"I did," she confirmed.

"The thought of committee work goes right to your head?" he joked, his smile going crooked and so, so sexy.

"I think it does." She played along rather than say that it was him who'd gone to her head.

Which meant that she really was getting carried away, and she knew it.

But not indefinitely.

She'd thought a lot about this since Sunday. She hadn't been able *not* to think about it most of the time. And the truth was that she wanted him so much that she just had to have him.

But only for right now. A little surrender without looking for tomorrows.

As long as she wasn't expecting anything more—no white dresses or wedding chapels or picket fences or bouncing babies—why couldn't she indulge the way Tyson did? The way Tyson had suggested she do in order to try to get it out of her system?

Because she just didn't know any other way she was going to get it out of her system.

That was what she'd concluded. Even before she'd accepted Derek's dinner invitation tonight.

The dinner invitation that had provided her with this chance.

And now here he was, and she had even less reason to resist, and even with the reasons that remained, she just didn't care. She still wanted him.

He moved a little closer on the couch, squeezing her knee and smiling devilishly. "If it helps cancel out that no, I can put you on the scholarship committee. And the arts committee. And the committee for animal rights.... You name it and there's probably a committee for it and I can put you on it."

"Oh, yeah—committees and committees and more committees—that gets me going," she joked in return, putting her hand on his thigh—about where it had been before she'd shied away on Sunday night. Or maybe an inch higher...

He was more serious when he said in a voice that was suddenly deeper, raspier, "You look sooo good, it's a shame to wreck it...."

"I kind of hate to ruin this, too...." she said, reaching with her other hand for the tie that was knotted meticulously at his throat and tugging on it.

"Go ahead, ruin it," he urged as his free hand went to the side of her neck and glided around to the back.

He pulled her forward to meet him as he leaned in and gave her a kiss that was so much hotter than the kiss he'd given her when he'd first come in. Hot enough to let her know that Sunday night had maintained its impact on him, too.

Gia did some multitasking, kissing him back as she untied his tie, slid it free of his shirt collar and kicked off her shoes.

When his tongue came to greet hers, she took off his suit coat and felt him unfasten his collar button to aid the cause of that kiss, their mouths going wider as the hunger that was only for each other ran rampant.

His free hand came to her breast, but only on the outside of her dress and bra, and that wasn't enough. It was something—something nice and arousing—but not enough. Not after she'd already learned the glory of having his hand on her without the filter of clothing between them.

She did some quick work undoing the rest of his shirt buttons so she could demonstrate, reaching inside once she could to lay her own hands on his chest.

Which was when she realized that that was the first time it had been bare to her….

And that it felt as glorious as it looked. Warm, smooth, sleek skin over muscles as solid as a brick wall. She couldn't resist going from the cut and carved pectorals down to the sharp six-pack of abs that led right to his waistband….

She just unhooked his belt and the button on his pants while she was there and then sluiced her hands around his waist to his back and up again.

That back that was oh, so nice….

His shoulders were big and broad and powerful and she filled her hands with the muscles there, massaging and mimicking what he was doing to her breasts, which were still locked in her bra and dress, her nipples trying their best to nudge their way out.

In spite of the fact that his shirt was beautiful, it was just in Gia's way, so she finessed it off him as her tongue parried playfully with his in a game that was growing ever more sexy.

And that was when he took his hand from her breast, his other hand from her nape and found the dress's zipper.

His mouth was wide over hers as the zipper went

down, as he spread the back of the dress and unhooked her strapless bra, too.

But as his hands went to her shoulders to take the dress off, it occurred to her somewhat belatedly that they were in her living room, it was still daylight so the drapes were open, and that they might be visible through the picture window.

Which meant that this needed to be taken to the bedroom.

And if she did that, it also meant that there was no turning back....

But that only gave her a split-second's pause before she plied the tip of his tongue with the tip of hers in one parting tease and ended the kiss to take his hand in hers and tug him to his feet.

He smiled when she did, apparently knowing what she was doing, going along willingly into her bedroom, where she'd already pulled the curtains in order to dress for tonight.

Still, bright September sunlight shone through, and Gia knew how much she wanted this when the fact that she was about to be undressed with Derek without the cloak of darkness didn't daunt her. Instead, she was just glad for the opportunity to see him when she took him to the foot of her double bed and turned to have a look at that torso, those shoulders, those biceps, that flat belly and the dark line of hair that went from navel down behind the waistband she'd left unbuttoned.

And as fantastic as he'd looked in the suit, what was underneath it was even better....

He used the hand she held to yank her to him, catching her mouth with his again in a wildly abandoned kiss that made everything that had happened in the living room seem tame. He continued what he'd begun there as he took off her dress, leaving it and her bra to drift down around her ankles.

Lace bikinis and thigh-high nylons—that was all she had on when he deserted her mouth for a look.

A look that adored and relished and came with a groan of approval as he took both breasts into both hands and recaptured her mouth with his.

Again her knees really did go weak in that first grip of big, gentle hands, of fingers that tenderly dug into her soft flesh, of palms where her nipples nestled impudently.

As if he knew he'd taken the starch out of her legs, one hand left her breast so he could wrap that arm around her and brace her as he went on kissing her into oblivion.

But not so far into oblivion that she didn't realize he was still partially dressed. And that she didn't want him that way.

So she did some unzipping of her own and let everything he had on from the waist down join her dress on the floor.

And then she wanted a look….

So she coyly escaped his kiss and took one.

Wow all over again….

Clothed, the man was something.

Naked, he was something else….

Hard and honed everywhere, he was the image of masculine perfection.

But he only let her have a brief glimpse before he swept her off her feet and tossed her good-naturedly onto the bed.

He joined her there, sitting on the edge and reaching for his slacks to take his wallet out and get protection—giving her a prime view of his divinely brawny back—

before he turned toward her, set the condom aside and put his full attention on her again.

His mouth took hers once more, his hand reclaimed her breasts and the other curved over her head to play with her hair as one thick thigh rested atop hers.

Gia let her hands go exploring. Exploring the expanse of those shoulders she just couldn't get enough of. The dip of his spine. Muscles and tendons that fanned from there. Tight derriere. The back of that thigh that pinned hers. The front of that same thigh. Then higher still than she'd gone before until she found that part of him that she'd only gotten a brief glimpse of.

The moan that rumbled in his throat let her know how much he liked it when she circled him with her hand. When she learned all he had to offer and teased him just a bit.

Just enough to put things into another gear.

He tugged with careful teeth on her lower lip. He kissed her chin, the hollow of her neck, and then he replaced his hand at her breast with his mouth and drove her just a bit crazy, too, sucking and nipping and running the tip of his tongue around the oh-so-sensitive outer circle of her nipple. Flicking at the eager nipple itself. Drawing her well into that hot, moist mouth that seemed to have the power to perform miracles. Miracles that awakened sleeping needs that had never been quite that demanding before.

And then he shifted up another gear when he slid his free hand down her stomach and inside her bikinis....

Her neck arched, pulling her shoulders right off the mattress when he first found her, his long, thick fingers easing into her. Slowly. Tenderly. Just asking permission for more to come later....

Her grip around him tightened in response, and that

brought a sound that was part laugh, part groan from him just before he withdrew his fingers and made her panties disappear.

Then his mouth returned to hers as his hands worked the condom, and more than his thigh rose over her.

Gia opened her legs to him as he came between them, his hands on either side of her shoulders, bracing his weight, his mouth finding her breasts again—one, then the other, flicking her nipples with his tongue and tormenting her with ever-increasing need—as he rediscovered that spot he'd made friends with moments before, slipping into her gradually, carefully, tenaciously.

Sound escaped them both when he reached his destination and she could feel him fully inside of her—long and thick and hard—where he stayed embedded and motionless, as if he was relishing it, too.

But only for a moment before desire took rein and he began that primal, fantastic trip. Slowly out and in again. And again. Each time with more speed. Each time diving deeper. Each time bringing more and more awake in Gia to make her blood rush, her heart race.

Her arms were around him, her hands splayed on that back that seemed like it could bear the world, as she matched his pace, meeting him with her hips, tightening around him then releasing as they found their rhythm and harmony.

Faster he went, and so did she. Working together in finely tuned unison. Bodies asking and answering instinctively until everything inside Gia grew and gathered and then couldn't be contained no matter how hard she tried.

Bursting wide-open, ecstasy thrust her into a space where she had no control and could only be carried away with it, by it. Carried away into an exquisite paradise where he waited for her. Where he exploded, too, holding her to cushion the blow and meld them together so tightly she didn't know where she began and he ended and the only thing she knew for sure was that she wanted it to go on and on and on....

And it did. Blessedly on and on until it spent itself. Then ebbed. Easing them down a little at a time, as they clung to each other in a meshing of more than bodies....

"Leave it to you to do dessert first," Derek joked after a time of just lying there atop her, catching his breath, kissing the side of her head.

Gia could only smile at his jest, too exhausted for a retort.

"Are you okay? I didn't break you, did I?" he asked then.

Gia laughed and realized she was going to have to find some strength to assure him. "Not broken, no. Are you?"

He flexed inside of her again. "Parts seem to still be in working order."

"Thank goodness!"

"You're telling me."

He didn't move, though. He stayed where he was, at home in her, it seemed.

At some point in the aftermath, Gia's arms had fallen away from him to the mattress, and now she wrapped them around him again, rubbing his back and absorbing all the sensations she could.

"I think we missed our reservation," he said then.

"You had some reservations? It didn't seem like it...." she teased him, playing with the words.

He laughed and nuzzled her ear, then sighed and whispered, "It was too good to be true."

Which was what she'd thought earlier.

What she still thought of him....

"It was," she whispered in return.

"I think we'd better give it a second test to be sure."

Gia took a turn at laughing. "Is that what you think?"

"It is. After a rest...."

He came out of her then and rolled to his side, his big body still half covering hers, one arm canopied over her head on the mattress again, the other across her chest much the way his thigh was across hers.

"What do you say?" he asked then. "The sun is going down.... We can try it in the dark now that we know the way...."

"I'll think about it," she said.

"Good," he answered, pulsing against her hip temptingly. But his voice had drifted and after another kiss to her temple, she could tell he'd gone to sleep.

Which beckoned to her, too.

But she fought it for a moment.

She just wanted to lie there with Derek as her blanket, enjoying the afterglow.

And all too happy with the thought that he would still be there when she woke and they could do this all again....

Chapter Ten

"Why did we only take half the day off?" Derek moaned when he came up behind Gia. He slid his arms around her waist to pull her back against him and nuzzle her neck.

They'd both called in to work and said they were taking Thursday morning off. It had seemed like a necessity after being up all night making love. Although part of the morning had been spent that way as well, rather than catching up on sleep.

"Maybe we should just take the afternoon, too," he suggested.

It was almost eleven. When Gia had finally gotten out of bed she'd put on the first thing she could reach—his shirt. That was all she was wearing to make coffee.

Derek had followed her into the kitchen after pulling on what had remained of his clothes on the bedroom floor. His chest was bare and even though Gia was fac-

ing the counter, she could see his reflection in the side
of the toaster. And that was enough.

She melted against him, tipping her head to one side
to allow him free access to her neck, closing her eyes
and wanting to go back to bed with him so much it was
as if they hadn't made love at all yet.

"I have a meeting with the owner of the company,"
she reminded. "He's coming in from Fort Collins just
for that. I have to be there." But there was nothing she
wanted more than to climb back into bed with Derek.

Which was beginning to worry her all on its own....

Making love hadn't had the effect she'd thought it
would. It hadn't taken wanting him out of her system the
way it was supposed to. It hadn't been the kind of freeing release Tyson had claimed it would be.

Instead, every minute with Derek had just made her
want him even more.

And more. And more. And more than before....

And now not only was she facing that, she was facing the fact that his car had been parked out front all
night, so Tyson would have seen it. And so would Larry
and Marion.

Plus, the cold light of day was forcing her to face some
other things, too....

"How 'bout I buy the company and then I'll be your
boss, and we'll hold all of our meetings in bed," he joked.

"Harry Cooley would never sell out."

Derek grumbled and nibbled on her earlobe. "Okay,
okay, okay..." he sighed. "We'll work this afternoon.
Then maybe we can actually get to dinner tonight. Before we start all over again...."

Gia wanted to do that, too. But that was the problem.

If she didn't stop this now, what was she in for? That
was what she'd started to ask herself as she'd made coffee.

Being with Derek all night long, making love, sleeping with him on and off had already gotten her in deeper emotionally than she had been. If she kept this up, she knew she'd get in even deeper. She'd be all the way in.

And then what?

Where would—where *could*—this go for her? she asked herself.

And the answer to that was *nowhere*.

Which, she realized, was the worst of what she had to face.

So she took a steeling breath and forced herself to wiggle out of his hold, moving away from him to the opposite side of the kitchen.

"I..." With the second steadying breath she wondered how she was going to do this. "We..."

"Yeah, I know—we have to go to work," he complained. "But my head is *not* going to be in it—I'll just be watching the clock and counting how many more hours have to pass before I can get back here."

"No," she finally managed. "That isn't what I was going to say. I was going to say that we...*this*..." She made a waving motion with her hand that included them both and what was between them. "We can't do *this*...."

Derek frowned in confusion and fell back against the counter. "This?"

"Everything. Seeing each other again. Dinner. What we did last night...and this morning.... We can't do any of it after this." And why did her gaze drop to his naked chest and make her yearn just then to start all over right this minute and make a liar out of her?

"I'm confused...." he said, as if she'd told a joke he didn't get.

Gia forced her eyes to his face—that face that looked

impossibly good even scruffed up with morning beard—
and thought that this was all hard for her to believe, too.

But it had to be done.

"I have to look at the big picture," she told him.

"The big picture," he repeated.

The big picture. That it was only a matter of time before she woke up and found herself head over heels in
love with a man who also woke up and realized that she
wasn't colorful or outrageous or wild or unique enough
to keep his interest.

That it was only a matter of time before she woke up
and found herself head over heels in love with another
man whose enormous family came first. Another man
whose strongest attachments and loyalties were to that
enormous family. Another man whose enormous family might not have the same kind of skewed practices
and principles as they once had had, as the Grants had,
but who no doubt could and would close rank against an
outsider like her if things didn't work out.

Or that it was only a matter of time before she woke
up and found herself head over heels in love with a man
who was with her for the wrong reasons. Who had met
her at a time when he was trying to please and appease
that enormous family that was so important to him by
denying his penchant for the kind of colorful women
who had so recently caused them all embarrassment.

But she couldn't say all of that so she said, "I'm fresh
out of a marriage...." Which was also true. "And so are
you—"

"There's nothing even remotely alike in the end of
your marriage and canceling out what I did in a drunken
stupor in Vegas."

"There is a little," she insisted. "I came out of my
marriage knowing what I do and don't want. You came

out of yours thinking you want to break old habits and turn over a new leaf."

"Okay, I guess those aren't too different," he conceded.

"But there are things that come along with you that are like what I just got out of and I don't want to get wrapped up in those things again. And I don't think I can be that new leaf that you may or may not be able to stick with...."

"And you're not willing to give it a little while to find out?"

"A little while and...it would just make it harder," she said softly, unwilling to reveal too much of how she already felt about him. "You said yourself that *regular* girls always end up boring you. And you know that because your family keeps throwing them at you and you try to like them to please your family, but eventually you just lose interest—"

"Yeah, I said that."

"Well, there's nothing unique or weird or colorful about me, Derek. So it stands to reason that given a little while, you'll want a rule breaker or a line crosser or..."

She stalled and shook her head. "I'm not any of the things you look for—that's the reality. I'm an ordinary, everyday person, and that isn't what you've *ever* wanted. But your family is as important to you as Elliot's was to him, and that carries weight—nobody knows that more than me. You want to please them, to be in their good graces, and instead the Las Vegas wedding shook the foundations. You're rebounding from it—I get it. You need to compensate for it. Atone for it. You want to prove you can clean up your act.... But I can't risk—"

"That I could be using you to make myself look good?"

Gia flinched. "I didn't say that. I don't think that's something you'd do consciously.... Is it?"

"No, it isn't."

"But I know how things work in a family like yours—if Elliot had done something that his whole family came down on him for, the way yours disapproved of the Las Vegas wedding, Elliot would have stopped at nothing to make it up to them. To redeem himself—"

"So you think my being here now, with you—liking you—is just me proving to my family that I can be a good boy?"

"Like I said, not consciously. But yes, I think it's possible." *Likely...*

"And you figure that once the dust settles I'll look up and it'll just be ordinary, everyday you who I brought in because it made my family happy, and what, Gia? I'll put you on a display shelf like your ex did and forget about you?"

Yes.

But she didn't want to say it like that, so she chose to be more diplomatic. "I don't want to risk it. And I also don't want this to get to the point where things have gone so far that we can't come back from them. That *I* can't come back from them. You said you still need some help from me with Larry and Marion, and they have too much at stake. I need to be able to call you or see you without it being awkward or ugly or... I need it not to hurt...."

"Because there isn't a doubt in your mind that that's where it'll end up—me hurting you? And what else? Are you thinking that I'm a Camden, and if things between you and I end I'll pull out of helping the Bronsons? Or do worse to them, like your former in-laws would?"

"No, I hope not. I'm just thinking that if this goes on—"

"It doesn't have a chance in hell of working—that's

what you're thinking. And that when it bombs, the Bronsons could end up collateral damage."

And me, too....

"I'm thinking that if things end later rather than sooner, it would make it hard for us to work together."

Because it would be impossible for her to be anywhere near him or even hear his voice without breaking down.

Which she was oddly close to doing already, just saying what she was saying.

"So you want to get out while the getting is good," he summed up.

What she wanted was him.

But only if *she* was what *he* wanted—ordinary, everyday her.

Only if she could be sure he would go on wanting ordinary, everyday her forever.

Only if she could be sure that he didn't merely want her *because* she was ordinary and everyday, as a path to redemption. A path that would be a dead end for her.

And since she couldn't be sure of any of that on top of everything else, she knew she had to shut this down. And she had to shut it down now or she wasn't going to be able to shut it down at all.

"I just think that to be safe, we need to take this back to it only being about Larry and Marion," she said, wondering how she was going to actually do that.

"After last night?" he demanded with more disbelief.

"Especially after last night," she said so quietly it was almost inaudible. "Even one more night like last night and…it'll get out of hand and complicated and that's not good for anybody, and it isn't what I'm ready for."

"So we'll keep it *un*complicated. We'll make sure—"

"I can't do that," she insisted, sounding slightly panicky. "I thought maybe I could—that's what got me into last night. But now I know…it's complicated for me no matter what…. So no. No more now. Last night was a one-time thing. We go back to me just being the go-between with Larry and Marion, the person who lets you know when their needs change down the road."

Her voice had risen an octave and was forceful enough to leave no question that she meant what she said. But still she felt compelled to add, "I mean it!"

For a moment Derek stared at her, frowned at her, stunned. Then he said, "I don't know what to say. There's no way I saw this coming, not after last night."

"Say we can go back to this just being about Larry and Marion," she repeated.

"I want to say that Larry and Marion, and *this*—" he mimicked her earlier gesture "—are two completely damn different things."

"But they're intertwined."

Even if they weren't, she just felt as if she had to protect herself. From Derek. From her own feelings for him. She felt as if she'd gone too far out of the safety zone she'd built around herself after her marriage and she needed to scurry back into it before it was too late.

"So this is it?" he asked, sounding dumbfounded. Then he shook his head in hard denial. "No, it can't be— things were too good…. I know you weren't faking it."

"No, I wasn't faking it," she said, trying madly not to cry and not understanding why she was on the verge. "It was…amazing."

Too amazing. Too good. It hadn't freed her, it had pulled her in the way Tyson had worried it would, and now she knew she had to get out while she still could.

"It was amazing," he parroted. "So you want to leave me wanting more? Is that it?"

She didn't want to leave him at all.

But being left wanting more herself was part of what she was afraid of. Which could happen if this wasn't real for him. If it was just something temporary, if it was just his attempt to prove to his family that he was sorry.

"I'm not playing a game," she told him. "I'm not trying to leave you wanting more. I just think it's better if it doesn't go any further."

"For the Bronsons' sake?" he said dubiously.

"And for mine...." she admitted quietly.

"So that's it?" he asked, disbelief still in his voice.

"I think it just has to be," she said, holding her ground.

"Fun while it lasted?"

Get in, hook up, get out—that was what Tyson had said.

Gia shrugged in answer to Derek's question, feeling at a loss and knowing suddenly that she'd been wrong when she'd told her friend she could do this.

"You didn't think it was going to be white dresses and wedding chapels and picket fences and bouncing babies, did you?" she said, trying to sound glib and hating that she heard an undertone of hope in her own voice.

"I hadn't thought that far."

"I can't let it get to where I do."

She looked at him again—the sight stabbing her through the heart because he looked so excruciatingly good to her—and said, "So let's turn back the clock."

"Twenty-four hours?"

"At least...."

"And we're just two people with one goal—to keep two other people together to the end?"

"Yes."

"I hate this, Gia. I don't know if I can do it...."

"You can," she assured him. "You wouldn't go back on your word, would you?"

"I wasn't talking about the Bronsons," he said. "I will do everything I said I would for them—that's not and never will be at issue."

"And that's all there can be to it," she said with finality. "This—" she waved her hand between them again "—was just…one of those things—something that happened along the way. And now needs to end."

Then she pushed away from the cupboard she was leaning against. "I'll change into something else and give you back your shirt."

His brow was a mass of lines—he looked as if he didn't know what had hit him, and didn't seem to have any idea what else to say to her as Gia left him standing in the kitchen and went to her bedroom.

But seeing that rumpled bed where everything had been so, so good all of last night and this morning cost her. Tears came flooding.

And she couldn't let him see that.

So she opened her bedroom door slightly, took off his shirt, hooked it on the outer knob and closed the door again.

Then she pressed her back to the wall beside the door and closed her eyes, just listening to him go.

I've lost my freaking mind….

That was what Derek told himself as he parked across the street and four houses up from Gia's place on Sunday night. He was positioned with a view of her house and the Bronsons', just hoping to catch a glimpse of her.

I'm worse than a crazy teenager. I've turned into her stalker.

And yet he didn't drive away. He shut off his engine and stayed where he was, staring at Gia's house and thinking the worst of himself.

It was just after dark. He'd left his grandmother's dinner and it was as if his car had driven itself to University Boulevard rather than home.

He hadn't heard from Gia since Friday when she'd called to tell him she'd convinced the Bronsons to accept all he and his family wanted to give them, that she'd spoken to the bank and taken the Bronsons there afterward, that the title papers on the house had been signed and so had the signature cards on the account he'd set up.

Her voice had been a little soft, a little shaky, but otherwise just businesslike. Until he'd asked if they could talk. Then she'd said a clipped "not about anything but Larry and Marion," and hung up.

And he was a damn mess.

He hadn't slept in the three nights since he'd left her.

He couldn't concentrate on work.

Television couldn't keep him from thinking about her.

He'd eaten very little because no food he could think of sounded good.

The one night he'd tried booze to get himself to sleep he'd just ended up drunk and morose and then had a hangover the next day.

And today, after not even being able to focus on a Bronco football game, he'd gone to GiGi's for Sunday dinner, where he'd been through-the-roof miserable.

How could he have been anything else when so many of his siblings and cousins had turned into such ridiculously happy couples! And remembering the past Sunday dinner when Gia had been there with him, he'd wished so damn bad that she was with him tonight that he couldn't wait to get out of there.

He'd begged off dessert, and since he'd been so quiet and withdrawn all through the evening, his grandmother had decided he must be coming down with something and encouraged him to go home to bed.

But bed was his torture chamber now, and instead here he was, parked a few houses away from Gia's, wondering what he was going to tell everybody if he got arrested for loitering or stalking or something.

What the hell is going on with me?

He hadn't ever gone through anything like this.

He'd been dumped a few times before, but it had never affected him this way. He'd always taken it in stride. In fact, he'd always seen it coming and actually been on the verge of doing the dumping himself, so it had saved him the trouble.

But this? This was something else. Something different. This was extreme....

As he watched Gia's house, the porch light at the Bronsons' place came on and caught his eye. He trained his gaze there, hoping Gia might have been visiting the elderly couple and was leaving.

He could feel his pulse gain speed at just the thought, and he began instantly to consider whether or not to intercept her if she did. To try to get her to talk to him now....

But it wasn't Gia who came out of the house next door to hers. It was Larry and Marion. Dressed in sweat suits—Larry's a plain heather-gray but Marion's a more flashy silver and purple—they were each carrying a bowl they took with them to sit on the chairs on their porch.

Ice cream. Derek thought they were probably having a bowl of ice cream before they went to bed. Enjoying the end of summer warmth of a September night.

They hadn't had an easy life, those two, he thought, feeling bad about his family's part in that on top of how bad he felt in general. But they had each other, he reminded himself. They still had each other.

And Gia was right; more than merely having each other, they did seem to still care for each other and enjoy each other's company, because there they were, talking and laughing when Larry stole a bite of whatever it was in Marion's bowl, then held out his own to offer her a taste of his as consolation when she put up a fuss.

God, he really did need some sleep when just the sight of that made his eyes sting.

And all he could think was that he'd give anything to be sitting on the porch next door to the Bronsons with Gia, just like that.

Just like that....

His own thought surprised him a little.

All that the Bronsons were doing was sitting on their porch, eating something, keeping each other company the way they had for seventy years. And that was what he wanted?

No boundary pushing? No line crossing? No rule breaking? No novelty in any way? Just sitting on the porch? Talking? Playing around like they must have a million times before? *That* was what he wanted?

But yeah, it was, he acknowledged with surprise. And a little skepticism.

Was he really envying something that plain and simple?

Pre-Gia, he certainly wouldn't have been. He'd have thought that it was nice for the Bronsons, but that it would be mind-numbing for him.

So why was he not only *not* thinking that, but wishing it was what he had?

It struck him as very weird.

And what made it even weirder was that if he imagined himself in that situation with anyone he'd ever met other than Gia, it didn't appeal to him at all.

A lifetime of Sharon the psychic? Of Celeste the head shaver? Of Carol the food police? Of Lila the statue?

Not a chance.

Not any more of a chance than with Brittany or Reagan or Nancy—the *regular* women who hadn't kept his interest as long as Sharon, Celeste, Carol or Lila.

But plug Gia into the picture and everything lit up like a neon sign for him.

Maybe Louie knew what he was talking about....

Because it had been the Camdens' handyman who had suggested that the strange women didn't keep his interest any more than the normal ones did. But that the *right* woman would....

He hadn't been sure *any* woman ever would. But all of a sudden here he was, realizing that he hadn't lost a drop of interest in Gia no matter how much time they were together. That it was the opposite, in fact—the more he got to know her, spend time with her, learn about her, the more he wanted to know. The more interested he was.

The more interested and enthralled and captivated and fascinated. The more charmed...

And yet she wasn't unusual at all.

But still he'd found even the small workings of her mind intriguing—her inventiveness, how she decided what to eat, her innovations for helping the Bronsons. It was nothing big, but it had left him with half a dozen instances since he'd met her when he'd wondered what she might think of something, how she might look at it differently than he did, what she might see in it that he didn't, how she might think to improve on it.

He just liked the way her brain worked. Somehow he'd discovered excitement in that. More excitement than he'd found in all the edginess and strange stuff with other women.

She surprised him in small ways—nothing elaborate or showy, nothing with any kind of shock value. Silly things like a simple comeback remark. The fact that she was obsessed with chocolate but ate vanilla ice cream. Nothing wild or bizarre, just things that were the tiniest bit out of the ordinary that made him feel like he could never be too sure what might come next....

He didn't know what Larry had said to Marion as he went on watching the two of them, but the elderly woman gave her husband a teasing little kick.

Moving with surprising speed, the geriatric Larry caught her ankle, bent over and kissed it, making both of them laugh.

There was still a spark there—Derek could even see it from where he was. And it helped him understand why Gia felt so strongly about not letting anything separate them.

Which made him think that there was also something so appealing—and even sexy—about that understated fierceness Gia had shown for her cause, about the energy she'd put into saving them, about how much she cared.

Again, it wasn't banner carrying or picketing or loud protesting—it had just been donation jars and a savings account and her yard sale and hard work getting the word out, and yet he admired her methods more than anything that had come before her.

He admired her....

And the longer he sat there thinking about her, watching the Bronsons and feeling the way he did, the more he knew that he just wanted to be part of a couple like they were, as long as the other person could be Gia.

Gia, who he suddenly knew was that *right person* Louie had talked about.

Gia, whose passion and sexiness were understated, too, until they were unleashed in the bedroom.

But Gia had shown him the door....

With good reason, he admitted then.

Because even he had thought she might be a subconscious overcompensation for the Vegas debacle. A sharp recoil from that to someone who was the exact opposite.

Even he had thought that when that recoil subsided he probably wouldn't be so infatuated with her. That he might revert to his old pattern and lose interest in her....

"God, you're an idiot," he said to himself as he realized that what he felt for Gia wasn't just infatuation. It wasn't about what had happened in Vegas.

He'd fallen in love with her.

That was why it was the way it was—the way she'd said it was between Larry and Marion. That was why it didn't take anything big or flashy or freaky for her to light up a room for him. All she had to do was walk into it.

That was why he thought every tiny detail about her was so special and intriguing and brilliant.

That was why it didn't matter to him that the wildest thing about her was her hair.

That was why he was going out of his mind without her.

And that was all why he had to get her back.

If he could....

The thought that he might not be able to sent him into a tailspin.

She'd stopped everything cold.

She hadn't given him even a hope for things to go on.

She wouldn't even talk to him on the phone about anything except the Bronsons.

The Bronsons...

Who were sitting on their porch at that moment.

Who she just might listen to if he could get them on his side....

Had he found enough favor with them to get *them* to play go-between with Gia?

He was afraid he hadn't.

But at that point he was willing to try anything.

Anything!

He had to.

Because suddenly he knew that the rest of his life was at stake. That Gia was the only one for him. And that if he couldn't convince her of that, he was never going to have what the Bronsons had.

So he restarted his engine, waited for a break in traffic and moved from his watching spot to park at the curb partially in front of the Bronsons' house and partially in front of Gia's.

Hoping *this* didn't get the hose turned on him....

Chapter Eleven

"You're having Larry and Marion get you in my door?"

When Gia's doorbell rang Sunday evening, she was surprised to peer through her peephole and see her elderly neighbors on her front porch.

And that was all she'd been able to see through her peephole.

Of course, she'd opened her door to them instantly.

Which was when she saw Derek standing at the bottom of the porch steps behind them.

"I figured if I could convince them, maybe they'd help me convince you," he said, coming up to join the Bronsons.

"Convince me of what?"

"We think you should hear him out, sweetheart," Marion said before he could answer her question.

"We saw his car out here the other morning," Larry contributed.

Gia had been grateful that they hadn't mentioned that before. Tyson had. But not the Bronsons.

"We know you, Gia," Marion continued. "We knew when we saw that that we were right about you—you're taken with this man. And we know you've been putting on a cheery face for us, but we can see you've been sad since he hasn't been around—"

"We blamed him—" Larry added, still easily falling into his old familiar criticism of the Camdens.

"But he says it was you who kicked him to the curb—is that right?" Marion asked.

"I didn't… I just thought that for all our sakes… Yes, it was me.…" Gia stammered her admission under her breath because she was embarrassed to have to be talking even in a roundabout way about the night she'd spent with Derek. The night that had unleashed too many things in her and caused her to suffer horribly without him ever since.…

"Well, we've heard him out and we think you should, too," Marion concluded.

"But if you need us we're right next door. And you know I can come running if I have to," Larry said with a still-not-completely-trusting glance out of the corner of his eye at Derek.

"Just talk to him," Marion encouraged. "Then, if you still want to hand him his walking papers, go ahead. But hear him out first."

The elderly woman took her husband by the arm then and turned him away from the door, tugging him toward the stairs.

"Right next door," Larry said over his shoulder, but Gia wasn't sure whether it was a reminder to her or a warning to Derek, who was now standing in front of her looking as tired as she felt. Though not as puffy eyed as she was from crying instead of sleeping since she'd sent him away....

"There's nothing to say," she told him when the Bronsons were headed next door again.

"I have a lot to say," he insisted firmly. "A lot to say that I just figured out—and if it helps, part of it is that you were right."

"Then why do we need to talk?" she asked. She didn't think she was strong enough to listen to him confirm that it wouldn't have worked out between them. It was bad enough having to go through what she was already going through without adding to it by hearing it from his own lips.

Lips she wanted to be kissing, in spite of everything, and was suffering with the knowledge that that would never happen again....

"You need to hear me out because you *were* right— past tense—to think what you were thinking. But now that I've had some time to come to grips with myself and what's really going on with me, to open my eyes... you aren't right anymore."

About which part? He still had a huge family to appease, a huge family he was intensely loyal to, and he still had a pattern for the kind of woman he wanted.

So Gia remained standing on her threshold, blocking his way, staring at him and wishing things were different but reminding herself of the realities that had caused her to send him away in the first place.

"Do I have to bring Larry and Marion over here again to get me in the door?" he threatened.

"I can't believe you talked them into getting you this far," Gia said, because while she'd persuaded the Bronsons to accept all the Camdens were doing for them, they still had hard feelings about the past. They wouldn't have conceded had she not convinced them all over again that what they were getting was nothing more than the Camdens owed them. That it was restitution they were rightfully due, and that Derek had admitted as much to her.

"They brought me here because they believed me when I told them what I just want the chance to say to you."

Gia continued to study him and keep him cooling his heels on her porch as she argued with herself.

She trusted the Bronsons, so if they'd brought him to her, they had to have felt that what he had to say was worth hearing.

And even though she didn't want to feel it, there was also hope—however fruitless it might be. Hope that there was something—anything—he could tell her that could fix things....

She sighed and swiveled so that her back was to the inside door, her arm outstretched to keep the screen door open, freeing a path for him to pass in front of her and come in.

He did, the scent of his cologne wafting to her along the way and making her wilt and pray for the strength not to give in to just anything that might mean she could be with him again....

Once he was inside, she closed the door and stood with her back against it, watching him again as he moved several feet into the living room before he turned to face her.

Why did he have to look like that? she bemoaned silently. Because even appearing as if he hadn't slept any more than she had since Wednesday night, he was still a sight for her very sore eyes in gray slacks and a black sport shirt that made him look dark and dashing.

And here she was in a pair of old jeans and a double layer of tank tops—gray over white—with her hair haphazardly pulled up into a ponytail to get the unruly curls out of her face.

"I just came from GiGi's Sunday dinner," he began. "I couldn't get past hating that you weren't there with me. And I also couldn't help thinking that if you said to them what you said to me on Thursday about being with you just to please them, it would have made them all laugh and scoff. It would have caused an uproar. Because I'm the last one in the family who'd do anything just for that reason. And I'm sure—especially after Vegas—that they wish I would."

"Maybe subconsciously you are," she suggested.

"Not subconsciously, not unconsciously, not consciously. When it comes to you, I might as well be an orphan, because nothing to do with you has *anything* to do with them. So take that off the table right now!" he commanded.

Gia didn't say anything to that.

"And you need to get something else straight about my family," he continued. "Yes, I'm loyal to them. But when any one of us partners up or starts a family, *none* of us expects to take priority over the relationship—"

"In an emergency—"

"A flat tire is not an emergency," he said, referring to the story she'd told him about her ex-husband. "And even in an emergency there are lots of us—whoever is available would show up. But if you didn't need me and I was the one running to help them, I'd drag you along so I could have you with me—because I'd *want* to have you with me, I wouldn't want to do it alone."

That carried weight for her. Leaving her behind was something Elliot had done whenever he'd answered any call from his family, emergency or not. Nothing would have pleased her more than if he'd actually wanted to have her by his side. He just never had.

"And when any one of us *chooses* someone," Derek went on, "that someone becomes family. So completely that I'm willing to bet you that of all the people you met last Sunday there's at least one or two you think were born Camdens who weren't…."

He was wrong. She knew exactly who the Camdens were and who among them weren't.

But she also knew what he was getting at because the more she'd thought about that dinner a week ago, the more she'd acknowledged to herself that spouses and fiancés of the Camdens were not treated the way spouses and fiancés of the Grants had been. That even she hadn't felt as much like an outsider with them as she had among the Grants right to the end of her marriage to Elliot.

"I know that your family *now* is different than the Grants," was all she said to that.

"But even though you were dead wrong about the family stuff," he went on in a more peacemaking tone, "it was reasonable for you to look at my history and figure there was some cause for concern about where my taste in women has led me before. To worry that it might lead me there again…."

If the Bronsons had gotten him in her front door so he could tell her she was right to stop things from going any further between them because she wasn't his type, she wasn't sure she'd be able to forgive them. Because she wasn't sure she could bear to hear him say it.

"There's just one really, really big factor that you couldn't have known about," Derek continued. "You couldn't have known about it because I just realized it myself…."

Gia raised her chin in question, steeling herself for the worst.

"I never actually had a weakness or proclivity for bad girls or rule breakers or psychics or zealots or weirdos in general. It's that their...colorfulness...offered enough of an extra to cover up the fact that I didn't actually feel much for them. A little attraction, sure. But that's all. So what their oddity or fervor about things did was fill a gap. They provided a few thrills and chills— entertainment—that distracted from the fact that I could take the women themselves or leave them. And with the few normal women... Well, there was nothing to cover up the fact that I could take them or leave them, so I—"

"Left them," Gia concluded fatalistically, still afraid he was acknowledging that she was in that category.

"That makes it sound worse than it was. My interest in them just ran out quicker," he amended. "But tonight— after being so down since Thursday morning that I've been pathetic, when I was actually parked down the street just hoping to be able to see you through your window or on your porch or in your yard—it came to me...."

He shook his head as if he couldn't believe he'd been so dumb.

"It came to me when I compared how I feel about you with how I felt about each and every one of the women I've dated or been involved with. It came to me that I've just never had strong feelings for any one of them. There was just more of a charge if there was something else going on with them."

Gia wasn't sure she'd heard him correctly. For all she knew, hope was skewing her understanding.

"How you feel about me?" she said softly.

And then he told her.

He told her about watching the Bronsons on their

front porch. About seeing for himself what was between them. About wanting that for himself. Wanting it with her and only with her. About how and why every little thing about her gave him chills and thrills. About how she fascinated and interested him. Endlessly...

"And it isn't even just what I already know about you," he went on. "It's that I can't wait to see what will come next—what you might do, what you might say, the way you might look on the beach at sunset or bundled in ski gear on top of a mountain. I can't wait to see you pregnant. I can't wait to see how you'll be as a wife, as a mom, as a grandma and a little old lady...."

Just the thought of that made him laugh and take a step closer to her before he said, "I love you, Gia. You're my Marion...."

But could he be her Larry?

"I have to think...." she said.

"Think. All you want. I'll wait. But I'm not getting out of here," he said, planting one hip on the arm of her couch to prove it. "It was too hard to get back in. Larry and Marion weren't easy to convince."

Because of what they thought of the Camdens in general, Gia surmised.

But in thinking that, she could honestly say that she believed the current Camdens weren't unscrupulous or unethical the way the Grants were, the way previous generations of Camdens had been.

She'd watched all Derek had done for the Bronsons, she'd tested and followed up to check out everything he'd claimed and promised and arranged, and she hadn't found that a single thing he'd said or done was anything but what it appeared to be.

Regardless of who or what had come before him, he was trustworthy. He was a man of his word.

And if he was a man of his word, then maybe she could believe him when he said that her appeal for him did *not* lie in the fact that she might be more acceptable to his family. That he wasn't trying to please them or make it up to them for having embarrassed them.

Which also meant that maybe she could believe him when he said that he would never put his family before her, too.

But what about the rest? The most important part of it all? Could his feelings for her keep him interested?

She didn't know. How did anyone ever know if someone they loved would go on loving them and finding them interesting?

That was the leap of faith that had to be taken, but she'd already taken it once and failed. And Elliot hadn't seemed like a risk at all....

Because Elliot had only shown her what he wanted her to see, she thought. About himself. About his family. About everything.

But when she thought about it, she realized that that wasn't true of Derek. Despite the fact that she'd worried about it, feared it, been suspicious, there hadn't been any subterfuge from Derek. And not merely when it came to the Bronsons.

He hadn't hidden anything about his past from her, including his history with unusual women and the trouble it had gotten him into.

He hadn't even hidden what he was most ashamed and embarrassed about—the Las Vegas wedding.

Instead, he'd been open with her. Honest with her even at his own expense. As open and honest with her as Larry and Marion were with each other.

No, there hadn't been any subterfuge, nothing superficial from him at all. Not the way there had been with Elliot.

So maybe she could trust that what was between them was real....

More real than what she'd had with Elliot.

But real enough to take a second leap of faith?

Somewhere along the way she'd dropped her head and stared at the floor, but now she raised her gaze to Derek, wondering...

But one look at him made her doubts begin to dwindle.

Because there he was, not only incredibly handsome and so hot she wanted to fling herself at him, but looking as if he'd been through the same kind of agony she'd gone through since they'd parted.

That wouldn't have been the case with Elliot—he'd have glided in making sure he looked his best to bowl her over. So it was actually preferable to see that Derek had suffered. It brought home to her that he really did have feelings for her. Feelings as intense as she had for him.

Because there he was, the man she'd come to see the merits of with her own two eyes, strong and powerful, promising to put her first—something Elliot would never agree to even when she'd pressed for it.

Because there he was, the man who had watched and listened and made sure that every little thing the Bronsons would ever need would be provided for them, the man who had started a foundation to help other people in their situation, because he was a caring, compassionate human being, not just to make himself and his family look good.

Because there he was, the man she loved.

She'd tried to deny it. To fool herself. But that was

the reason that sleeping with him had only gotten her in deeper.

She loved him. With all her heart.

And he was the one who made her want to become a wife again.

To become a mother.

He was the one she wanted to grow old with the way Larry and Marion had grown old together....

She took a breath, and he lifted his eyes to her face. His expression was full of hope, too. But also full of vulnerability—something else that only won her over all the more.

Then she pushed away from the door and went to him as he stood up as if to face sentencing.

"You're sure?" she whispered.

He smiled a smile that went straight to her heart. "More sure than I've ever been about anything. You *are* my Marion. If you'll just let me be your Larry..."

That brought tears to her eyes as she reached a hand to the side of his face, desperate just to drink in the warmth of his skin again.

"Marry me, Gia," he said then. "Say you'll marry me and I promise you I'll never stop kissing you until the day we die...."

She laughed and blinked back even more tears. "I'll hold you to that," she warned.

"You won't have to," he said, clasping his arms around her waist to pull her closer.

Then he did kiss her. Profoundly, before he stopped and repeated, "Say you'll marry me...."

It was all there in his eyes, in his voice—he wanted it from her as much as she wanted everything from him. He needed to hear her say it. Needed to know he could have what truly was his heart's desire....

"I will," she said without any hesitation now.

"And say that when I'm old and decrepit you'll rig my bed to fix whatever ails me," he joked.

"And when you're old and decrepit I'll rig your bed to fix whatever ails you," she pledged.

The small smile was replaced by a sober expression as his blue eyes delved into hers with pure sincerity. "I love you," he said quietly. "I love you more than any words can say."

"I love you, too. It's why I had to send you away Thursday—I loved you too much to pretend I didn't."

He nodded. "But don't do it again. I won't live through it."

"Never again," she vowed.

He kissed her then, and as Gia kissed him back her arms went around him and she let her whole body melt into his.

And just like that she knew.

She knew that there in his arms, their bodies fitted together flawlessly, was where she was meant to be.

Through good and bad.

From now until time stopped.

* * * * *

A sneaky peek at next month...

Cherish™

EXPERIENCE THE ULTIMATE RUSH OF FALLING IN LOVE

My wish list for next month's titles...

In stores from 20th June 2014:

❏ Her Irresistible Protector — Michelle Douglas

❏ A Bride by Summer — Sandra Steffen

❏ The Maverick Millionaire — Alison Roberts

❏ A Doctor for Keeps — Lynne Marshall

In stores from 4th July 2014:

❏ Million-Dollar Maverick — Christine Rimmer

❏ The Return of the Rebel — Jennifer Faye

❏ Dating for Two — Marie Ferrarella

❏ The Tycoon and the Wedding Planner — Kandy Shepherd

Available at WHSmith, Tesco, Asda, Eason, Amazon and Apple

Just can't wait?

Visit us Online
You can buy our books online a month before they hit the shops! **www.millsandboon.co.uk**

0614/23

THE
CHATSFIELD®

Enter the intriguing online world of
The Chatsfield and discover secret
stories behind closed doors…

www.thechatsfield.com

Check in online now for your exclusive
welcome pack!

Join our *EXCLUSIVE* eBook club

FROM JUST £1.99 A MONTH!

Never miss a book again with our hassle-free eBook subscription.

★ Pick how many titles you want from each series with our flexible subscription

★ Your titles are delivered to your device on the first of every month

★ Zero risk, zero obligation!

There really is nothing standing in the way of you and your favourite books!

Start your eBook subscription today at www.millsandboon.co.uk/subscribe

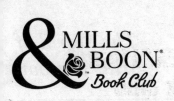 

MILLS & BOON® Book Club

Join the Mills & Boon Book Club

Want to read more **Cherish**™ books?
We're offering you **2 more** absolutely **FREE!**

We'll also treat you to these fabulous extras:

- 🌹 **Exclusive offers and much more!**

- 🌹 **FREE home delivery**

- 🌹 **FREE books and gifts with our special rewards scheme**

Get your free books now!

**visit www.millsandboon.co.uk/bookclub
or call Customer Relations on 020 8288 2888**

The World of Mills & Boon

There's a Mills & Boon® series that's perfect for you. There are ten different series to choose from and new titles every month, so whether you're looking for glamorous seduction, Regency rakes, homespun heroes or sizzling erotica, we'll give you plenty of inspiration for your next read.

By Request

Back by popular demand!
12 stories every month

Cherish™

Experience the ultimate rush of falling in love.
12 new stories every month

INTRIGUE...

A seductive combination of danger and desire...
7 new stories every month

Desire™

Passionate and dramatic love stories
6 new stories every month

nocturne™

An exhilarating underworld of dark desires
3 new stories every month

For exclusive member offers go to
millsandboon.co.uk/subscribe

Which series will you try next?

HEARTWARMING

Wholesome, heartfelt relationships
4 new stories every month
Only available online

HISTORICAL

Awaken the romance of the past...
6 new stories every month

Medical Romance

The ultimate in romantic medical drama
6 new stories every month

MODERN™

Power, passion and irresistible temptation
8 new stories every month

MODERN tempted™

True love and temptation!
4 new stories every month